Secrets of the Magic Ring

Secrets of the Magic Ring

Karen McQuestion
Illustrated by Vincent Desjardins

PUBLISHED BY

two lions

two lions

Text copyright ©2011 Karen McQuestion
All rights reserved
Printed in the United States of America

Published by Amazon Children's Publishing
P.O. Box 400818
Las Vegas, NV 89140

ISBN-13: 9781612181424
ISBN-10: 1612181422

For Jack, who believes he is my favorite

K.M.

To the memory of my mother and father,
who always encouraged my artistic pursuits.

V.P.D.

CHAPTER ONE

The best thing that ever happened to Paul was when his aunt offered to pay for a pool as a gift for his ninth birthday. Talk about a major development! His mother had choked on her iced tea when Aunt Vicky told them the news. It would be the best kind of pool too, one with a big water slide and a diving board.

At first it didn't sound like his parents were going to go for it. Aunt Vicky had been kind of mean in the past, making snide comments about the way their house was decorated. "Ticky-tack" was what she called his mother's new window treatments, little wooden shutters that Paul thought were really cool. Aunt Vicky could be kind of mean to Paul too. Sometimes she told him to scram when the adults were talking, and once she ordered him to go change his shirt. It was only a little dirty, and why did she care anyway? But his father nodded at him to do it, so he did. Aunt Vicky was as bossy as she was beautiful.

His parents told Aunt Vicky that they would consider her generous pool offer and get back to her. He overheard them discussing it when they didn't know he was listening.

His father said, "I don't care if she is rich. I still don't like the idea of accepting a gift that costs thousands of dollars. Who knows what she has up her sleeve?"

His mother had a different take on it. "Vicky seems different now for some reason. I don't think she has an agenda this time." They talked about it for a long time, and then Paul didn't hear anything about it for days. He'd almost given up hope, until one evening at dinner when they told him their decision. The answer was yes.

Paul jumped out of his seat in excitement. "Really? We're for sure getting a pool?" he asked. His voice came out in a little squeak like it sometimes did. He loved swimming, but the public pool was so far away that they hardly ever went. And now he'd have one in his own backyard! Wow.

His mom and dad grinned at each other, pleased with his response. "Really," his dad said. "The crew is coming next week to cut down some trees and dig the hole. It will be the first day of your summer vacation. You can watch them work from the house, but you can't go outside. You'd just get in their way."

"This is so great. Thanks, Mom and Dad." Paul ran around the table and gave them each a hug, then bounced on the balls of his feet before returning to his plateful of baked fish and potatoes.

"You and your friends won't be able to go in the pool without adult supervision," his mother said. "And none of that horseplay, that pushing you boys do. I don't want anyone to drown or crack their heads open." She worried about everything.

"I know, I know." Paul stabbed a chunk of roasted potato and nodded vigorously. "No horseplay. Got it, Mom." He couldn't wait. This was going to be awesome.

CHAPTER TWO

*T*he first morning of summer vacation, a crew came to dig the pool, and Paul invited his friend Celia over to watch. Celia was a year older and his closest neighbor. Her house was on the other end of their country road. Paul and Celia often played together in the woods behind their houses. Today they sat cross-legged on the floor and peered through the patio door. Front-row seats for the excavation. When Paul's dog, Clem, plunked down next to them, Celia rubbed his floppy ears and petted his furry back. "What a good boy you are," she said. The dog yawned and stretched his legs contentedly.

The previous day the pool had been mapped out and stakes inserted in each corner. Yellow tape linked the stakes and outlined the edges. Paul had walked around the perimeter trying to imagine how it would be when it was finished. Today his dream would become a reality.

Through the glass, Paul watched as the crew of men wearing orange vests and hard hats yelled directions back and forth. They began by cutting down trees with chainsaws. The trees came down quickly, faster than Paul would have thought.

"Complete carnage," he said excitedly.

"Poor trees," Celia said. Her blonde hair framed a frowning face. "They probably had no idea that today would be their last day. That's so sad."

It was just like Celia to think about how the trees must feel, when really, who cared? The main thing was that Paul was getting a pool! He bounced up and down, almost upsetting the bowl of pretzels by his knee. "Yep," he said, "sometimes trees have to die if you want to get a pool."

Two of the men dragged the branches away to the wood chipper in the driveway. Paul's mother went outside to ask if she could have the wood chips for her garden, while Paul and Celia stayed in their spots. Now the digger was in position. One of the men waved to the two kids as he pulled the tape off the stakes.

Celia waved back and Paul did too, and then the digging began. The engine growled, and the machine scooped into the dirt, looking like a giant metal jaw eating crumbly chocolate. The men's voices were drowned out by the sound of the digger.

All morning the two kids sat and watched, mesmerized. The space was transformed from a backyard of grass and trees to a deep hole with piles of soil and rocks alongside it. The digging part of the project would take two days, Paul's parents had said. The first day to make the hole, the second to shape it and make it exactly right for the other workers who would create the liner for the water.

After lunchtime, Paul reluctantly left his spot by the window when Celia's mother came to pick them up. Celia's folks owned a toy company called Lovejoy World. Today was the debut of an exciting new product, and Celia and

Paul were invited to watch the ceremony at the factory. Paul had visited the company before with Celia, and it was always fun. Usually the employees fussed over them and gave them treats, and invariably he came home with some free toys. Today, though, he found himself wishing he could stay home to watch the action in his backyard. What if he missed something? Man, it seemed like nothing happened in his life for years, and now he had two things happening at once. There was no point in changing his mind about going with Celia, though, because his mother would say he was being rude and then push him out the door.

At Lovejoy World he managed to forget about the pool for a short time. Celia's dad unveiled his newest toy creation, the Lovejoy Magic Wand Flute Necklace, and all the workers oohed and aahed when he demonstrated how it worked. "What do you think, Paul?" Celia's father asked afterward.

"Awesome," Paul said, politely faking enthusiasm. "It looks like a lot of fun." The Magic Wand Flute Necklace was clearly a girl thing, but the lights that sparkled when the flute played were pretty cool.

When Celia and her parents dropped him off at home a few hours later, he went straight to the backyard and stared down into the hole. The piles were now gone, and there were deep tread marks all over the grass. His mother wouldn't be happy about that.

The back door swung open, and Paul heard the screen door squeak. "Oh there you are," his mother called out. "I didn't know you were home."

"They just dropped me off," Paul said. "I wanted to see what happened while I was gone."

"You didn't miss much," Mom said. "It took a little longer than they thought because they hit what they think was an old well a few feet down. It made such a racket I nearly got a headache." She narrowed her eyes and furrowed her forehead in worry. "You're making me nervous standing so close to the edge, Paul. Move back a little bit."

"I'm not going to fall in," Paul said, but he stepped back anyway, just to humor her.

"We're eating soon," she said. "Why don't you come inside now?"

"I just want to stay out for a few minutes." Paul toed at the dirt and knocked a stone down into the pit.

"Have it your way." She sighed. "Just don't get too close to the edge, and whatever you do, don't get dirty." She went inside, and the screen door slammed shut.

Paul couldn't keep his eyes off the hole. He had no idea it would look so impressive, like a miniature Grand Canyon in his backyard. He leaned over, cupped his hands around his mouth, and yelled, "Hello down there!" then waited, but there was nothing. No echo, no answer. He knew his mother would be furious, but something made him sit down by the edge and dangle his feet into the opening. It made him feel like an explorer. Or maybe one of those guys who digs for dinosaurs and stuff. What was that called—an architect? Or was he confusing the word with the title for people who design buildings? Anyway, the main thing was the digging and discovery. Who knew, maybe his backyard held gold nuggets or skeletons. Anything was possible.

The yard smelled good, like the woods after a rain. The dirt in the hole was the color of brownie mix. When he craned his neck, he could see all the way down. No sign of an old well. They must have dug it all out.

Paul leaned forward, pressing the heels of his feet against the side of the pit for support. It was then he spotted something about halfway down, jutting out of one side. It appeared to be more square than round, so he didn't think it could be a rock. So odd. Why would there be a box-like structure buried in his backyard? He tried to get a better look, but it was impossible to see at this distance. He needed to get closer.

He stood up and brushed the dirt off the back of his pants. All he needed was a spade from the garage and he could dig it out. His parents wouldn't like it, but if he was really quiet he might be able to do it without them knowing. There was no point in asking—they'd just say no. He remembered something his grandpa had once said: "Paul, it's easier to ask forgiveness than it is to get permission."

His mother had gotten mad then and responded sharply, "Don't tell him that!" Then she turned to Paul and said, "Grandpa is kidding. You *always* need to ask permission." His grandfather had winked at him when his mom wasn't looking. His parents were big on the rules, but Grandpa was cool.

The back door swung open again, and his mother startled him out of his thoughts. "Paul, please come in and wash up. We're eating in ten minutes."

Paul knew not to argue. Later he'd go into the hole and figure out exactly what was sticking out of the dirt.

CHAPTER THREE

*A*fter dinner, without being asked, Paul helped his mother clear the table and rinse the dishes. He knew from past experience that this was an excellent strategy for putting her in a good mood. Now for sure she'd let him go outside without any questions. While he and his mother finished with the dishes, his father settled down in front of the TV, just as Paul had hoped.

When the kitchen was spotless, Paul said, "I want to go out for a while, okay, Mom? Maybe see if Celia can play?" His mother approved of Celia, so mentioning her name was a nice touch. Of course he'd said "maybe," so it wasn't a complete lie.

His mother smiled. "I suppose it'll be fine. But stay in the neighborhood, and once it starts getting dark, come on home."

"I will," he promised.

"I don't want to be yelling for you and calling over at the Lovejoys' house. You're old enough to keep track yourself."

"I know, I know. Stay in the neighborhood, and come in once it starts getting dark," he said, reciting the words back to make her happy.

She hung the dish towel over the oven handle. "All right then, Paul."

From the next room, his father called out, "The show is starting, Leah."

"Be right there," she said.

It was all too easy, Paul thought, slipping out the back door. He went to the garage and found the small spade his mother used for gardening. He noticed that the ladder, which was usually up in the rafters, was leaning against the wall by the lawn mower. What luck! Paul moved it carefully so it wouldn't make any noise. He knew his parents were engrossed in their show, but if they heard a big bang in the garage they'd come out to investigate, and that would be the end of it for him.

The aluminum ladder was easy to lift. When he got to the backyard, he glanced back at the house, worried his parents might be able to see him through the window. Lucky for him, Mom had closed the shutters, probably to keep the glare out of the room.

Paul lowered the ladder into the hole. It was a bit short, and the top only came to the edge of the opening. He could make it work, though. Paul pushed on the ladder to check for stability. If the thing fell over while he was on it, that would be terrible, the worst thing ever. And if his mother found out what he was doing, she'd probably never let him out of the house again.

He rested a foot on the top rung of the ladder, and it held fast. He really was going to do this! Paul took a deep breath.

All was quiet, except for the sound of birds chirping from the direction of the woods. Must be careful, he thought.

So many times he'd bungled things by hurrying. The kids in his grade called him Spaz because he was always jiggling and bouncing. He tried not to, but honestly, he couldn't help it. Energy coursed out of him like an electrical current. His mother often said she'd like to have half of his stamina. She had a serious nap habit and was known to fall asleep in the recliner while watching TV. That would never happen to Paul, who loved moving around and was never bored. He was so full of ideas he sometimes found it hard to sleep at night because his mind swirled with possibilities.

And now another possibility was in front of him. If only the kids at school could see him now. He stuck the spade in the waistband of his shorts and lowered himself down the ladder. One rung at a time, that was the way to do it. When he got to the part where the mystery object stuck out of the side, he realized the ladder was positioned too far to the left. Shoot!

He climbed out of the hole with regret. It was hard to move the ladder from the top, but he maneuvered it back and forth to the right spot. Another trip down, one footstep at a time. When he was alongside the bump, he reached over to touch it. It was rectangular in shape, about the size of his dad's tackle box, and encrusted with dirt. So weird that it was underground, whatever it was. He tapped on it with the spade, but it didn't budge, so he starting digging around it. Man, oh man, this was cool! And to think his mother thought he was at the Lovejoys' house right now hanging out with Celia. Celia never would have climbed down into a hole. She wasn't the explorer type at all.

He periodically stopped digging in order to shimmy the box from side to side, but even after several minutes, it wouldn't come out. Paul considered getting a shovel, but he knew it would be hard to manage and still keep his balance on the ladder, so he kept going with the spade and used his hands too.

After digging some more, the box loosened enough that Paul thought he could pull it free. He wiped the spade off with his fingers and rested it on a rung of the ladder, then grabbed the box with both hands. Almost there, almost there. He wiggled it back and forth, like a loose tooth.

And finally, with one last yank, it popped out. The force caused the ladder to tilt slightly, and he panicked. A last-minute shifting of his weight wasn't enough. The ladder went sideways, and Paul went with it. He plunged downward, dizzying and fast.

Bam! Paul hit the bottom still holding the box.

CHAPTER FOUR

"Ouch," Paul yelled. He sat for a moment, stunned, the wind knocked out of him. He felt a sharp stab, but despite the pain, Paul felt a huge sense of accomplishment. He'd done it, and all by himself too. If only the kids at school could have seen him, digging like a real explorer, like a, what was the word? An archeologist, that was it! At last he remembered. Who was the spaz now?

He grinned to himself. The box, encrusted with dirt, felt solid in his hands. Bigger than a shoebox, it was wrapped in the middle with some kind of belt or strap. Buried treasure, that's what he'd found!

Paul stood up and put the box under one arm while he lifted the ladder back into place. He made his way up to the top, slowly, because he was carrying the box, and carefully, because his butt hurt.

Getting out of the hole would be tricky. The ladder was the most wobbly at the top, and he didn't want to fall again. Paul set his free hand on the top edge to steady himself and was startled to see a pair of brown shoes in front of him.

Tilting his head back, he saw a strange boy standing directly above. The boy looked older than him, and he had long, stringy-looking hair and shabby brown clothing. "Need some help?" the boy asked, extending his hand.

Paul looked nervously at his house, wondering if his parents knew this stranger was in their yard. He said, "No, I think I have it."

"Let me take the box for you," the boy said. "It'll make it easier for you to get out."

Paul tightened his hold. "No thank you. I'm not supposed to talk to strangers."

The boy laughed. Paul thought it sounded like a mocking kind of laugh. The boy said, "I'm not a stranger. I'm your neighbor. My name is Henry. I used to live right there." He pointed to the woods. "I know all about your family."

"Could you move over, please?" Paul said. "I need to get out."

Henry leaned over, his hands on his knees. He frowned at Paul. "Take my hand," he said, "and I'll have you out in no time."

Paul had a very bad feeling about this. Where were his mom and dad when he needed them? What kind of parents watched television while their son was being threatened by a stranger in the backyard? "No, I don't need your help," he said firmly. "And I think you should go. I don't know you, and my mother wouldn't like it if you were here."

Henry said nothing, but narrowed his eyes in a mean way. And then he stood up. Paul was relieved, thinking he was leaving, but then Henry said, "GIVE. ME. THAT. BOX. NOW," in a truly terrible voice that sent chills down Paul's spine.

Paul looked at the box and up at Henry, not knowing what to do. And then something happened. His dog, good old goofy Clem, came bounding of the doggie door and right over to the stranger. Usually Clem loved everyone. Paul's dad said he'd probably greet a burglar with a friendly slurp of his tongue, but Clem didn't like this boy. As he got closer, he growled and bared his teeth in a menacing way, like a dog possessed.

Henry backed away, a look of fear crossing his face. "Don't think this is over," he said to Paul. "I'll be back." And then he ran off into the woods, disappearing from sight.

Paul's heart pounded. Clem came up and looked down at him, barking enthusiastically. "Shh, quiet, boy," Paul said, looking nervously at the house and back at the woods, where the strange boy had gone. Clem danced in circles and yapped again. Paul scrambled up the ladder and out of the hole before his parents looked out the window or Henry returned.

Who was that kid, and what did he mean when he said he'd lived in the woods? As far as Paul knew, there were no houses in that direction. The woods went on for a long, long way, and ended at a busy highway.

Thinking about what Henry had said made him shiver. The boy's tone was so threatening. He clearly wanted the box, so it must contain something valuable. But how would Henry even know what was in it?

He decided at that moment not to tell his parents about Henry. Telling would mean sharing the whole story—the digging, the ladder, the box. They'd certainly want him to hand over what he found, and he didn't want to do that.

It was his discovery. He should be the one to open it. And would they even believe that a strange boy had been in the yard? In the moments since he'd left, the encounter seemed unlikely even to him. It felt like waking up from a dream and trying to figure out what was real.

He needed to put the box somewhere safe, and he also needed to put away the ladder and spade, and he couldn't do both at once. Paul left the ladder in the hole and went to the garage, where he hung the spade back on its hook. He rooted around in the garage until he found the tarp his father used when painting. He recognized the yellow splatters as being left over from the last room painted, the bathroom off his parents' room. Aunt Vicky called it the "lemon bathroom," which was kind of funny, but his mother didn't think so. He wrapped the box inside the tarp and set it on a shelf next to his father's tools before going back for the ladder. Clem trotted next to him every step of the way. Such a good dog! He was going to get a treat tonight. He rubbed Clem's head in appreciation. "You saved my life, you good dog. I love you, yes I do." Sometimes he acted like Clem was a pest when Celia was around, but the truth was, the dog was good company. And sometimes Clem was the only one he could talk to. A dog could be your best friend in a way a person never could.

He yanked at the ladder and pulled it out of the pit by walking backwards until it lay at his feet. Easy as can be. He felt better once the ladder was back in the garage and he'd locked the door. What a relief.

He was hosing off his hands in the backyard when his mother opened the door. "Paul? Is that you?" Her head popped out. "Oh, it is you. I wondered why the water was running."

"Just cleaning up, Mom." He held up his hands to show her. "I didn't want to come in with dirty hands."

"That's my boy!" she said. "I guess you do listen to me." Clem nudged at the door with his nose, and she let him in. "After you're done, come on in. It's getting late."

"Okay, Mom." Really it wasn't that late. It wasn't even close to getting dark. More likely his parents' TV show was over, and she wanted to know Paul was home for the night. She had a thing about everybody being in, so the house could be locked till morning. Paul wasn't going to make a fuss about it. He'd had a close call and wanted to go indoors where it was safe anyway.

He finished washing up and went inside. He desperately wanted to retrieve the box from its hiding place in the garage, but it would have to wait until the time was right. His mother was always watching, and there was no way he'd be able to get a dirt-covered object into the house without her noticing. Yes, he'd just have to wait.

CHAPTER FIVE

*P*aul didn't get a chance to go out to the garage that night. Once again, being an only child worked against him. It seemed like his mother monitored his every move. Much as he wanted to go out and sneak a peek under the tarp, he knew not to chance it. Instead, he went through the usual motions of playing video games until she told him it was time for bed. Obediently, he turned off the game, washed up, brushed his teeth, and got into his pajamas.

As he headed off to bed, his mother called out to him. "Paul?"

"Yes?"

"Come here a minute."

His heart sank. Oh no, she knew. Had she looked out the window and seen something? "Okay, Mom." His feet dragged as he retraced his steps.

She pulled him into a hug and kissed the top of his head. "I just wanted to tell you that I love you and I appreciate that you've been acting so mature lately. Coming home on time and cleaning up without being told. I'm just so proud of you."

He felt so guilty he didn't squirm out of her grasp like he usually would. This could be his chance to confess, to tell her everything about the box and the boy, Henry, but he just couldn't do it. He heard how pleased she was and didn't want to spoil things. "I love you too, Mom," he said, and she hugged him even tighter.

From behind them, his father said, "Don't suffocate the boy, Leah."

She released Paul and cupped his chin. "Just keep up the good work, Son."

"Okay." He turned to go back up the stairs and stopped on the landing to call out, "Good night, Mom and Dad."

Together he heard them say, "Good night, Paul." He felt safe and loved. The doors were locked, and Clem was on guard. No one could enter the house, and no one knew where he'd hidden the box. Everything was going to be fine. And tomorrow he would get to find out exactly what was in it. It would be like Christmas, only better.

* * *

While Paul slept, the wind blew and the trees in the woods behind his house made a whispering noise. Jasmine, the Watchful Woods fairy whose job was overseeing his family, made note of all that had happened. Fairy magic allowed her to make suggestions to people and animals, and she had used this magic to send Clem outside to scare off the strange boy. Being new herself, she had no idea what was in the box, but she was sensitive enough to know that big changes were afoot.

Her wings fluttered as she thought of all that had happened that day. The boy, Henry, had seemed menacing, but she'd handled it fine, she thought. He said he'd be back, though, so that was worrisome. And right now Henry was camping in the woods, which was odd, but at least she could keep an eye on him and figure out what he wanted. Perhaps she should ask Mira, her boss, for advice? No, that would be admitting she was incapable. And she wasn't. She would monitor the situation and take care of anything that came up.

* * *

In the garage, the box, still wrapped up in the tarp, rested comfortably on the shelf. To the casual observer it would appear to be just a dirt-covered box, but inside, where no one could see, the box was awakening. It had been underground waiting to be discovered for a long time. Finally, finally, the magic inside the box would get to make its way out into the world.

CHAPTER SIX

*T*he next day, Paul leapt out of bed. Clem sensed something was up, and he followed Paul around into the kitchen, his fluffy tail wagging. "Big day, huh boy?" Paul said, patting Clem on the head. He'd been talking to Clem more and more lately, and sometimes he caught Clem giving him an understanding wink or nod in agreement.

Paul's mother, who usually micromanaged his schedule, seemed to have relaxed her standards. Maybe she was in summer vacation mode, or maybe it was because Aunt Vicky was giving them the pool, but lately she'd been smiling a lot more and nagging a lot less. When Paul asked if he could play outside, she said, "I'd love to let you, Paul, but you know the crew is coming today to work on the pool, and I'm afraid it wouldn't be safe for you. You can watch from the window, though, if you like." This last sentence she said brightly, like this would make him happy.

"Sure, the window is good," Paul said. Then thinking fast he asked, "Is it okay if I go out in the garage? I wanted to pump up my bike tires and clean the spokes." He'd never pumped up the bike tires in his life, and he wasn't even sure if people cleaned spokes, or why they'd want to. Still, it seemed like a reasonable lie, and he was proud of coming up with something so quickly. Very sly on his part.

His mother tilted her head to one side, considering. "Yes, I guess that would be fine. Just don't leave anything lying around. When your father comes home, he'll want to pull right into his space."

"I know, I know," Paul said. "I won't make a mess."

And the matter was settled.

A few minutes later, the workers arrived and his mother went outside to talk to the foreman. He saw them talking in the yard, his mother pointing to the hole and the man gesturing and smiling. They seemed to be agreeing on some finer point. Mom nodded and then stepped back while the men got all the equipment in place. Having his mother momentarily distracted was nice, but he knew his time was limited. Eventually she'd open the garage door to check on him, and he'd better be doing something with his bike or she'd be asking questions.

Paul filled a bucket with water and grabbed a few rags. Clem looked up with interest. "Coming with me, Clem?" he asked. The dog uttered a low whine that Paul took for a yes.

In the garage, Paul pulled his bike away from the wall, set the pump next to the tires, and draped one of the rags over the seat. If he heard the door starting to open, he had everything in place and could act like he was working on his bike.

The next step was getting the box out of its hiding place. He pulled the tarp out and breathed a sigh of relief when he saw the box still nestled in the center, just where he'd left it.

Paul put the box next to the bike, then folded up the tarp and returned it to the shelf. Clem walked in circles before settling in next to the bike to watch.

Ideally, Paul would have liked to run the box under the hose, but he was afraid that would ruin it. Also, his mother always noticed when the outside water was on. She didn't miss a thing. So instead he dipped a rag into the water and wiped at the dirt. He worked quickly and scrubbed hard, and soon the surface was uncovered.

Whoa! The box looked like a pirate's treasure chest complete with curved top and metal handles. More scrubbing revealed that the piece wrapped around the center was a strap held together by a buckle. He repeatedly dipped the rag in the water and rubbed at the box. The water turned a murky brown, and still he worked.

He heard his mom's footsteps before she even opened the door, and he was ready for her, hiding the box behind his back and grabbing a clean rag to swipe at his bike spokes.

"Paul?" She craned her neck to get a look at him. "Everything okay out here?"

"Everything's fine, Mom." He did a bit of playacting, pretending to be engrossed in shining up the bike spokes. Oddly enough, they did seem to need a good cleaning. The back wheel even had a cobweb along one side.

"Is Clem getting in your way? I can bring him in."

Clem gave Paul a look that said, *Please no, don't let her take me away. I want to stay with you.* "Clem's fine out here," Paul said, and Clem thumped his tail in appreciation.

"Okay then, I'll be doing laundry if you need me."

The door closed, and Paul stopped working on his bike. "That was a close one, eh buddy?" he said before turning his attention back to the box. He carefully unbuckled the strap and set it on the garage floor next to him.

"This is the moment of truth, Clem," he said. "Now we get to find out what's inside." The dog scrambled to his feet to get a closer look. Paul lifted the lid, and the hinges creaked. His jaw dropped in amazement, and he turned to Clem and said, "Wow, will you look at that!"

CHAPTER SEVEN

*P*aul stared for a few minutes, taking it all in. The inside of the box wasn't quite what he'd expected. He'd hoped for a box full of treasure—diamonds and gold coins and rubies—but that's not what he got. Still, it was pretty cool. Instead of a jumble of valuables, there was just one item resting on a bed of dark black velvet. It was a gold ring with a sparkling blue gem in the middle. He'd never seen anything like it. Stuck in the middle of the ring was a rolled-up piece of paper. Paul pulled it out and smoothed it against the garage floor. The paper was as fragile as an autumn leaf and yellowed like the old papers he'd seen in the museum.

"What do you suppose this is, Clem?" he asked, but the dog didn't have an answer for him. The writing looked old-timey like when people used to dip pens into inkwells. Paul had difficulty reading the words. He wasn't the best reader at school, but he was stubborn and would stick with something if motivated. He was motivated now, so he struggled to work out the words, reading it aloud: "This ring bestows on the wearer their most fervently wished-for ability, even

beyond normal capabilities. One use per wearer." Huh? He turned it over, but there was nothing written on the back. "I wonder what that means. Kind of weird."

Paul picked up the ring. It was heavy and warm in his hand. He could feel some kind of energy radiating off the metal. Or was it just his excitement that seemed to make the ring vibrate? It was not a beautiful piece of jewelry. In fact, it looked clunky, but there was something very regal about it, like maybe it had once belonged to a king or queen. Probably a king because it looked more like a man's ring. He put the ring on his middle finger, and it fit perfectly, hugged his finger in fact. Odd, he would have thought it would be sized for adults. He took it off and tried it on his ring finger, and again it fit just right. Puzzling. He'd thought his middle finger was bigger. Oh well. He shrugged.

"What do you think, Clem, pretty cool?" he asked. If Clem had an opinion, he wasn't saying. Now that the contents of the box were revealed, the dog had settled into a lying down position.

What to do with the ring? Paul couldn't wear it at home because his parents would certainly want to know where he got it. Keeping this a secret was getting to be more complicated all the time.

Too bad school was out for the summer. Paul would have loved to have shown the other kids the ring and told them he found it digging underground. Maybe they'd have a new respect for him and stop calling him Spaz. Especially Brody, the worst human being on the planet. He made fun of Paul at every turn. Brody never seemed to leave him alone—always trying to trip him, stepping on his heels in the hallway, mocking him at the lunch table. Recently Brody had noticed that Paul sometimes talked to Celia, and after that he'd say loudly, "Oh, there's Paul's girlfriend," making obnoxious kissing sounds as he passed by. When Paul told his mother about this, she had downplayed the whole thing. "Well, Celia is your friend, and she is a girl, so he's sort of right. Don't pay any attention to him, Paul, and he'll get tired of teasing you." She was so wrong. Paul tried ignoring him for weeks, but if anything Brody only got worse.

Paul looked more carefully at the ring. Around the stone was a scrolled design, and inside the ring was some kind of etched writing. He squinted and peered intently but couldn't make it out. The letters were too small. He'd need to borrow his father's magnifying glass if he wanted to read it.

Paul put the ring and the paper in his pocket and wrapped the box back up in the tarp. He'd leave it there for the time being. Later, when he was sure his mother was busy, he'd hide it. He had discovered the perfect hiding spot a few months earlier when Clem was nosing around in his room. There was a floor vent in his closet that had never worked; it wasn't even hooked up to the furnace, according to his dad. When Paul pried the vent grate out, he stuck his arm down and discovered it ended in a flat surface. He'd decided then that it was the perfect place to stash things he didn't want anyone else to know about. Which was good because there was absolutely no privacy for a kid in his house.

Paul moved his bike and the pump back to where they belonged, and he gathered up the rags and bucket of water. Later his mother commented on how well he'd cleaned everything up. "You're getting to be the perfect son," she said with a grin. But he barely remembered much of anything he'd done after opening the box and putting the ring in his pocket because he was just too excited.

Later after he'd gotten his father's magnifier, he went to his room, took out the rolled-up paper, and pressed it flat. He reread it and tried to make sense of the words. He never was one to look up definitions, usually skipping words if he didn't know them, but this time was different. He looked up each unfamiliar word and then checked the sentence again, but it still wasn't completely clear to him. *Wearer* would be the person who wore the ring. That one was easy, but the rest of it was confusing. *Bestow* meant "to give," and *fervently* meant "with great intensity of spirit." Paul had an idea what a *wished-for ability* was, but the part about "beyond normal capabilities" was confusing. Still, it sounded like magic.

He stuck the ring on his finger and tried to think of a cool ability. He blurted out, "I wish I was invisible." He concentrated hard and closed his eyes for a minute, but when he opened them nothing had changed. What a rip-off. It wasn't magic at all.

He took out the ring and looked at the inscription through the magnifying glass. Enlarged it was much better. Now he could see the letters clearly, although they looked a little wavy, like reading them through water. He leaned in to look closer and saw that the letters spelled out two words. He read them aloud: "Be selfless."

CHAPTER EIGHT

*T*hat night when Paul was in bed, he slid his hand under his pillow to check on the ring. He'd put the note in the bottom of his desk drawer in between some loose-leaf paper. Even if his mom went on one of her cleaning frenzies, she'd never find it there. Later on, he'd put everything in his floor vent, but for now he wanted to keep the ring close at hand.

He pulled it out, slid it onto his finger, and imagined he was a king who could bestow favors upon disadvantaged visitors. Things would be different if he were a king. He imagined that sniveling idiot Brody kneeling before him begging for mercy because he'd committed some horrible crime. Normally he'd be sentenced to death, but if Paul was in a good mood that day he'd let him off with a lifetime of servitude. "Kiss my ring," he'd tell Brody, and gratefully Brody would. Ha, that would be the day. If only life were fair, things like that would happen. He slipped the ring off and tucked it into his pillowcase. Paul couldn't remember the last time he was this happy. In a week or so the pool would be finished, and he'd found this awesome ring in the meantime. This was going to be the best summer ever.

* * *

Outside in the woods, Henry paced. If it weren't for that stupid dog, he'd have the box by now and the ring would be his. It had been so close, he could almost feel it. He wanted the box; he needed it to finish this thing off. That boy Paul had no idea how powerful the ring was and all the trouble it could cause. Sure, it seemed like fun and games at first, but eventually it all went sour. His life was proof of that. Once upon a time, Henry had made a wish on the ring, one he regretted. Now he was all alone, not a friend in the world. If only he could fix this mess. He missed his family. He wanted to return to his old life.

The ring had once been his, and he wanted it back. Henry sat on a stump and plotted how to get it from Paul. The biggest risk was being found out before he had the ring in his hand, so he'd have to proceed with caution. For so many years, he'd waited for his chance. Soon, very soon, it would all be over.

CHAPTER NINE

*T*he next day, Paul took the box, the ring, and the rolled-up paper, and he put them into his hiding place in the vent. The next two days were filled with the excitement of the pool, so the ring stayed safely tucked away in his room. When the pool was completed, a truck came and filled the pool with water. Paul had thought they could fill it from the hose in the back of the house, but his parents had laughed at the idea. "Do you know how long that would take?" his father asked.

And his mother added, "That much water would empty the well, and then what would we do?"

The truck that delivered the water was a tanker. Once the pool was full and the truck had pulled away, Paul asked his mother, "Can I invite Celia over to swim?"

His mom said, "Oh I'm sorry, Paul. I thought you understood. We need to wait for the filter to work and the heater to warm up the water, and then tomorrow the guys from the pool service will come. They add things to the water to keep it sanitary."

It all seemed unnecessary to Paul. It was a hot day, and he was willing to swim in unheated water. "I don't mind if it's cold and not so clean," he said. "I can always take a shower after I swim."

But his mother held her ground. "We're having a pool party next Saturday," she said. "That's the first official day we can use the pool. We invited Aunt Vicky, and Celia and her family, and a few other relatives. If you want to invite a friend or two, you can."

Paul hated waiting. He was terrible at it, in fact. Normally he'd try to get her to change her mind. Sometimes if he followed her around the house and begged, she'd throw up her hands, give in, and say, "Have it your way!" He opened his mouth to say something contrary, but then thought better of it. "Okay, Mom," he said. "I guess I can wait a few more days. Maybe I'll invite Alex."

For some reason, it helped that he had the ring. At night, when his parents weren't around, he took it out of its box and put it on his finger. Before he went to bed he tucked it into his pillowcase so it would be close by when he slept. It made him feel better about life in general. Sometimes, just as he was falling asleep, he thought about the boy, Henry, who had demanded he give him the box. The memory of Henry standing over him was fading, and he was not afraid of him anymore. Paul was proud of how he'd told Henry to step aside and that he should leave. Paul had been bold, bolder than he usually was anyway. Maybe next year he'd stand up to Brody. He was tired of being picked on. Enough was enough.

* * *

Meanwhile, Henry spent his days in the woods trying to figure out a way to get into Paul's house. He knew the floor plan perfectly. Years before, he'd spent a lot of time there playing with his friend Silas McClutchy. That was sixty-some years ago, when it was Silas's house. He was certain he could still squeeze through the doggie door, a little swinging door built into the main door. The doggie door had been there almost as long as the house. Before Paul and his parents lived there, it was Paul's grandfather's house, and his great-grandfather before him. And all of them had dogs. The dogs had names like Rex and Laddie and Tipper. And now there was Clem, probably the dumbest of the bunch, but very loyal to the family. When he growled, Henry had been afraid.

Henry watched the house, hoping that at some point the family would leave for the day and take the dog with them. But someone was always home. And when he got too close to the house, Clem appeared out of nowhere and started barking like a crazy thing. The dog always seemed to know when he was around. How could that be?

"I need that ring," Henry said to himself. "I want that ring." He sat on a stump and put his head in his hands and cried.

* * *

Jasmine, the fairy girl, had been keeping an eye on Henry, always sending Clem out when he got too close to the house. Henry had been spying on the family, she understood that, and now she was spying on him. Her tiny size and speed worked in her favor. She flew so silently that he never even sensed he was being followed. She might as well have been a butterfly for all the notice he took.

She'd been worried about Henry at first. He'd spoken menacingly to Paul, but lately she was getting the idea that he wasn't a real threat. If anything, she sensed a sadness in this boy. She couldn't quite figure out where he came from or what he was all about, though. He didn't look much older than Paul, so it was puzzling that he was on his own. Didn't he have parents? Why was he dressed in rags and scrounging for food? He stole the stale bread that Paul's mother put out for the birds. Other times she saw him come back from outings with bags of junk food that he'd purchased from the gas station over on the highway. She'd wondered where he got the money until she saw him picking up cans to sell to the metal recycling company.

What a sad life for a child his age. She wasn't assigned to Henry. Paul and his family were her responsibility, and she'd been warned about getting sidetracked helping other people. "Worry about your own assignment. Concentrate on your family only," her boss, Mira, always said. "Other people aren't your problem." She knew Mira was right, but something about Henry made her want to break the rules. Someone needed to help him.

CHAPTER TEN

*T*he night before the pool party, Paul was so excited he had trouble falling asleep. Jittery and jumpy, he got up out of bed and pulled the grate off the vent to get the ring. Wearing it calmed him down; it had a soothing energy. He got back into bed and thought about the party. His mother was making all kinds of great food—fruit salad and pasta salad and lots of other salads—none of which had lettuce, now that he thought about it. Hey! That was kind of funny. He'd have to point that out to Alex and Celia when they came. He hoped Alex wouldn't think it was weird that Celia had been invited. He remembered how Brody had made fun of him and said she was his girlfriend. "I'll just tell Alex that Celia's my neighbor," he whispered to himself in the dark.

As his eyes felt heavier, he tucked the ring into the underside of his pillowcase. He liked having it near, but if his mom checked on him after he fell asleep he didn't want to risk her seeing it.

The party wouldn't start until late afternoon, which gave his mother plenty of time to do the frantic cleaning she always did before company came. "It's a pool party—aren't they all going to be outside?" his father asked, a big mistake on his part. She hated when they objected to her cleaning. Seeing her face, his father added, "I mean, I think the house looks fine already."

She handed him a dust rag and told Paul to empty the wastebaskets. Clem was banished to the basement where he would be out of the way and couldn't shed any more hair on the furniture.

Paul's mother was a whirlwind when she was expecting company, especially if it was Aunt Vicky, because she believed her sister judged her housekeeping and cooking. All morning Mom stayed busy, making salads, baking brownies, and arranging the paper plates and plastic silverware. Paul's dad was going to be grilling the hamburgers and hot dogs, which was a relief. If his mom was the one cooking, she'd probably have a meltdown. As it was, after she'd finished the obvious cleaning, she moved on to organizing closets and doing laundry, of all things.

"Leah, I don't think our guests will notice if we have dirty laundry," Dad said. "It's not like they'll be snooping around looking in our hamper." He pantomimed opening the hamper and pinched his nose at the smell. Paul thought it was funny, but his mom only smiled.

"I just feel better knowing everything is shipshape," she said.

An hour before the guests arrived, Paul's mom came out to the pool area where Paul and his dad were getting the grill ready. She walked toward them with her hand cupped and an excited look on her face. "Look what I found when I was pulling the sheets out of the washer."

"What is it?" Dad stopped to look.

She unfolded her fingers to show him. "It's a man's ring. I've never seen it before. Do you know where it came from?"

It was his ring! Oh no. How did she get it?

Dad took it from her, held it up, and examined it. "No, I've never seen it before. So odd. It was in with the wash, you said?"

"Yes," she answered. "I decided to quickly wash all the sheets in the house before our company arrived. The wash cycle had just finished, and I was going to put them in the dryer when I heard the clunk of something hitting the floor. When I looked down, there it was."

Paul had a sudden sick realization. He'd accidentally left the ring in his pillowcase. When his mother stripped his bedding, the ring must have come along with the sheets into the wash. Oh why hadn't he remembered to put it back in his hiding place?

"Huh." His dad's face scrunched up. "It looks kind of valuable. Where do you suppose it came from?"

Paul held his breath, thinking they'd ask him. He would have to tell the truth. It was one thing to avoid telling his parents things, but it was another to lie. He wasn't above avoiding the truth, but he wasn't a liar.

"I have a theory," his mother said. "You know that wicker basket I bought at the flea market?"

"Sure." Dad nodded.

"I was using it for the laundry. I wonder if it was already in the basket before I bought it and I never noticed. Then when I put the sheets in, it got mixed in. That's the only thing I can think of."

"Sounds like a reasonable assumption."

"What a find," his mother said joyfully. "I'm never lucky this way."

"We should have it assessed by a jeweler," Dad said. "I bet it's worth a lot."

Mom slid the ring on her finger. "I'm not so sure I want to sell it," she said. "I kind of like it, and it fits me perfectly."

Paul felt a little bit like throwing up. The ring was his discovery. He'd gone through so much to get it, and now his mother was going to wear it around the house? Part of him wanted credit. He opened his mouth to tell them the truth about the ring, but his tongue was lodged in his mouth. He stammered, "I, I, I..."

His parents looked at him in amazement.

"Are you okay, Paul?" Mom asked.

His father patted him on the back. "Do you need a drink of water?"

"No, it's just that—" And here his words were stopped and he couldn't say any more. What was stopping him? "The ring, I mean…"

"What about the ring?" his mother asked.

He couldn't seem to spit out the words to tell them how he'd found the ring. He knew his parents would be disappointed that he'd been so sneaky. They were watching him intently now. He'd have to come up with something. "Could I take it to school sometime, to show the kids?"

"Certainly not," Mom said. "It's far too valuable. I'd worry about it getting lost or ruined."

"We'll find something else for you to take for show-and-tell," his dad said. Paul was annoyed. He was going into fourth grade and hadn't done show-and-tell for years.

His dad leaned over to examine the ring on his mother's finger. "Leah, you might want to put that somewhere safe before everyone gets here."

"Oh no, I'm wearing it," Mom said. "It fits like a glove, and there's something about wearing it that makes me feel confident. It's very regal, don't you think?"

"Very regal," his father agreed.

Paul had a bad feeling about this.

CHAPTER ELEVEN

*P*aul was momentarily distracted when the guests arrived, but the thought of the ring was never far from his mind. His friend Alex arrived carrying a tray of cookies, which he handed to Paul's mom.

"Well, isn't this nice," she said.

"My mom says it's good manners to bring something," Alex said.

"Your mother sounds like a wonderful person," Mom said.

Alex just shrugged. "She's a pretty good mom. The cookies are really good too."

"Please tell her thank you for me," Mom said. "And now you boys can go in the pool if you want." And that was all they needed to hear. Paul and Alex tore off and cannon-balled into the water. Within a few minutes they'd tested the slide and jumped off the diving board. Paul's dad took pictures as if it were a historic event. "Boys, over here. Smile!" he said.

By the time the rest of the guests had arrived, Paul's fingers were like raisins, but he didn't care because he was having so much fun. When Celia got there with her parents and grandmother, Paul waved from the pool to get her attention. "I brought water toys," Celia said, emptying out a mesh bag onto the deck of the pool.

"Cool," Alex said. The boys looked over the assortment of balls and toys and decided to play with a small basketball hoop that fastened to the side of the pool. It turned out that Alex was fine with Celia being there. The three of them had the pool to themselves since none of the adults wanted to swim.

When Paul saw his Aunt Vicky, he swam over to the side and asked if she'd brought her suit.

"I don't swim," she said firmly, running her fingers through her gleaming hair. Celia once said his aunt looked like a supermodel, and today he agreed. Besides being tall and skinny, Aunt Vicky was dressed fancier than his mom, and her nails were perfectly polished.

"It's really nice and warm," Paul said politely. He thought it was a shame that she wasn't swimming when she was the one who paid for the pool. "I think you'd like it."

"No, you don't understand. I don't swim at all; in fact, I sink like a stone. I had a traumatic experience as a child, and ever since, I don't go in the water. Not ever. I even prefer showers to baths."

"Oh, that's too bad," Paul said.

Vicky pursed her lips. "It is too bad. I've often wished I could swim, but I know I never will. Thanks for asking, though, Paul. It was very sweet of you."

When his dad finished cooking the hamburgers and hot dogs, Paul's mom served lunch to the adults, then called the kids out of the pool.

"Everything looks really good," Celia said politely as she loaded up her plate with fruit salad, chips, and a hot dog.

"Well, thank you," Mom said. The grown-ups sat at tables set up alongside the pool.

"I have to say you've really outdone yourself, Leah," Aunt Vicky said. "Everything looks fabulous. And you look great. Have you lost weight?"

"I have lost a few pounds, thanks for noticing," Mom said.

"And where did you get that gorgeous ring?" Aunt Vicky asked. "I don't think I've ever seen anything like it."

Paul froze.

"I picked it up at a little antique store out in the country," Mom said. "I got quite a good deal." She turned her head and winked at Dad, who grinned. "I really like it." She held her hand out and admired it.

Aunt Vicky got up from her seat to get a closer look. "It's exquisite. I have quite a collection of antique jewelry, and I've never seen anything like it. How much is it worth?"

"I don't really know," Mom said. "I just got it, and it hasn't been appraised yet. Very, very valuable would be my guess."

Celia's Grammy, who hadn't said a word up until that point, got up from her chair to see the ring. "Incredible," she said, her eyes widening. "This looks exactly like a ring I knew of years ago. I was just a child at the time. I'd thought it was one of a kind. Where did you say you got it?"

Mom blushed. "At a little antique store out on a country road."

"Really." Celia's grandmother reached out to touch it. And then she spoke softly, as if to herself. "I thought I'd never see it again."

"It is unique," said another woman at the table. Paul knew she was his father's cousin, but he couldn't remember her name. Oh wait, it was Dora. Cousin Dora. His mother said Dora was full of opinions. Dora said, "I usually wear more delicate rings, but if you like bigger pieces it's quite distinctive."

"Well, I think it's beautiful," Mom said decisively.

"It is beautiful," Aunt Vicky said in agreement. "Is there any way you'd consider selling it to me?" she asked. "I'd give you a fair price. After you get it appraised, I mean."

"Oh no, it's not for sale," Mom said. "I really love this ring."

Paul's dad cleared his throat. "Why don't we just hold off on that idea? We might want to sell it in the future, but today's not the day to discuss it."

Mom gave him a sharp look. "I'm certain it's not for sale, today or ever."

"That's fine," Vicky said. "I don't want to cause trouble. I just thought I'd ask."

Mom smiled softly. "Would you like to wear it for a while?"

"Oh, could I?"

"Sure, but just for the afternoon."

"Of course," Aunt Vicky said. "I'll give it right back." Paul's mom handed over the ring. Aunt Vicky slipped it onto her finger and smiled. "Look, it just fits."

"It always fits just perfectly, no matter who wears it," Grammy said quietly. No one but Paul seemed to hear her.

Aunt Vicky held out her hand and admired the ring. "And it's the perfect weight. So many rings feel flimsy nowadays, but this one has some heft to it."

"Just for the afternoon," his mother reminded. "Then I'll want it back."

"Of course," said Aunt Vicky.

CHAPTER TWELVE

Vicky had just put the ring on her finger when Clem, still locked up in the basement, started yowling and barking in the most horrible way. From the patio Paul could see Clem's face through the basement window, and he knew the dog must have climbed onto the old sofa they kept in the rec room. All of the guests jumped when they heard the commotion.

"My goodness!" said Cousin Dora.

"What's wrong with Clem?" Celia asked. She and Paul exchanged a look, knowing that this wasn't typical for Clem. Now the dog was making short, explosive barks as if he were being tortured.

"Ken, would you go quiet the dog?" Paul's mom said to his dad. To the others she said, "I'm so sorry, I don't know what's gotten into him."

"You never know with dogs," someone said.

"Crazy animal," Dora said, shaking her head.

Celia's grandmother was still standing next to the pool-side table. Suddenly she gestured toward the back of the yard and shouted, "Look!"

Everyone turned their attention to see a boy slinking near the edge of the woods. Paul recognized him as Henry, the one who'd threatened him the day he'd gotten the box out of the hole. At this distance, the boy didn't look scary at all. His clothing—pants and a button-down shirt—was shabby and tattered. They looked to be brown in color, but that might have been because they were old and dirty. His hair was long and tangled like he didn't own a comb. The expression on his face turned to horror at being spotted. He froze for an instant, and then, like a deer smelling danger, he turned and slipped back into the woods.

"Henry, wait," Grammy yelled and walked in his direction. Unfortunately, she was heading straight for the pool. Paul saw it, but he wasn't close enough to stop her. Aunt Vicky was, though, and she quickly stepped in front of Celia's grandmother to block her way. Grammy charged ahead, bumping into Aunt Vicky. The pool deck was wet and slippery, and Vicky, losing her footing, fell backwards into the pool.

"Oh no, Vicky," Paul's mother stood up in horror. "She can't swim. Someone help her!"

Paul's father grabbed a flotation ring, but before he could even toss it into the pool, Vicky popped up to the surface laughing. "This is wonderful," she said. "The water is so warm, and I'm not even afraid anymore. Why didn't anyone tell me how wonderful this was?" And even though she was fully clothed, she flipped over to float on her back. "I was just wishing I could swim, and now I can. Oh, joy!" She turned then and did the front crawl, and then the side-stroke, and ended by doing some water ballet type–thing usually done by synchronized swimmers. She yelled happily, "I could swim forever."

The guests looked on amazed. "I thought you said she couldn't swim," said Cousin Dora.

"She can't." Mom looked on in disbelief. "She panics and sinks like a stone. Vicky almost drowned once, and she vowed never to swim again."

"I guess she got over it," said Celia's mom. "I used to be afraid to go on airplanes, but I worked my way through the fear. It's the power of the mind."

"No, it's the ring," Celia's grandmother said, but she said it so softly that only Paul heard. "Swimming must be her most fervently desired wish."

Everyone seemed to have forgotten about the mysterious boy in the woods. Everyone but Paul. He made his way over to Grammy and whispered in her ear. "Mrs. Lovejoy? You know the boy in the woods? You said his name—Henry?"

"Henry was a childhood friend of mine. I haven't seen him for a long time." Her face had a dreamy, faraway expression.

That didn't make any sense at all to Paul. "So this boy looks like someone you know?"

"Mrs. Lovejoy." Paul's mother came around to where Paul and Grammy stood and interrupted their conversation. "Why don't you come and sit down? I'd be glad to refill your drink for you."

"That would be very nice. Thank you," said Celia's grandmother.

In the pool, Aunt Vicky was still whooping and laughing. "Paul, why don't you and your friends join me? The water feels fabulous."

What happened to Aunt Vicky was crazy and hard to understand, but at least Clem had stopped barking.

CHAPTER THIRTEEN

The fairy girl, Jasmine, watched the party and puzzled over the turn of events. Who was Henry, and why did Celia's grandmother think she knew him? And how was it that Aunt Vicky could now swim? Celia's grandma thought it was because of the ring. Was that true?

Jasmine knew things were getting tricky. Looking after a family was a big responsibility, and it was all new to her. Her boss, Mira, said that Jasmine had a gift for keeping track of her humans and helping them through their everyday problems. This business with the ring was different, though. Clearly not the usual routine.

When the pool party wound down and all the guests except Vicky had left, Jasmine zoomed out of her hiding place and flew deep into the woods in search of Mira. She loved flying and was good at it, using the breeze to her advantage and avoiding birds and flying insects. Her wings were strong and shimmered when they caught the light. Jasmine was aware that humans should never see her, so she was extra careful during the day. Today, she flew to all of Mira's usual places: the underground spot she called home and the hollow trees where she sometimes counseled other fairies. Mira had a difficult job being in charge of the rest of them. Not everyone was as diligent as Jasmine. Some of the fairies were lazy and needed to be scolded on occasion.

That's exactly what Mira was doing when Jasmine finally found her. Boyd, the laziest fairy of them all, was leaning against a tree grinning impishly. He had a tendency to think he could get by on his charm and good looks. As if.

Jasmine hovered above them for a moment before landing a few feet away. She didn't want to intrude, but she needed to talk to Mira right away. "I mean it, Boyd," Mira said. "This is serious. One more slip-up and I'll demote you, understand? You'll be on trash patrol for a decade."

"I understand, Mira," Boyd said, but he was looking elsewhere as he said it. Jasmine wondered if he was paying attention at all.

"All right then, off you go," Mira said and gestured with a wave of her hand.

That's all Boyd needed to hear, and he didn't waste any time. He zipped away without looking back or saying good-bye.

Mira smiled at Jasmine. "Well, if it isn't my star pupil," she said. "What can I do for you, Jasmine?"

"There's trouble at Paul's house," Jasmine said. "I thought I could handle it, but as it turns out, I can't." She frowned. "There are a few things, really," she said. "There's a strange, homeless boy lurking about, and a ring that seems to have some magic powers, and the fact that Celia's grandmother seems to know about the ring and the boy. His name is Henry, and he's a lost soul, I can tell."

Mira listened intently as Jasmine poured out the details about Paul finding the box in the hole, his mother finding the ring in the laundry, and his aunt wearing the ring and suddenly being able to swim. Jasmine said, "I don't understand any of it, and I'm not sure what I'm supposed to be doing, if anything."

Mira sighed. "I know exactly what's happening. This all started way before your time, but I know all about the ring and its magic. I can explain everything."

CHAPTER FOURTEEN

*A*ll of the guests had left, and still Vicky was swimming. "I can't thank you enough for inviting me to your party, Leah," she called out while floating on her back. "I never would have known I was capable of swimming. And here I always thought I'd sink like a brick. Think of all the years of fun I've missed out on."

She stayed in the pool even while the family cleaned up the food and put away the pool toys. "I hate to spoil your fun," Paul's dad said at last, "but the party's over, and you really need to come out now."

Vicky reluctantly climbed up the ladder and took the towel Paul offered her. She looked back longingly at the water. "I suppose that next time I should bring my suit," she said.

Mom stood nearby, amused. "I have to say that I'm shocked at how well you took to the water," she said. "I haven't seen you swimming since the incident."

"I vowed never to get into any body of water again," Aunt Vicky said. "If I hadn't fallen in today, I would never have known I could swim."

"And how is it that you fell in the pool?" Dad asked. "I wasn't looking and somehow missed it."

Aunt Vicky dabbed at her wet clothing with the towel. "Celia's grandmother was going to walk right into the pool, and I darted out to stop her. That's what I was doing when I slipped and toppled into the pool."

"Celia's Grammy was distracted because she saw that boy out in the woods," Mom said. "I wonder who that kid was? He looked a mess."

"Probably just some kid from around here," Dad said. "Trespassing on our property. I can't say I like that very much. If he comes around again, we should make it clear that this is private property."

"Leah, do you have a change of clothes I can borrow?" Aunt Vicky asked. "I can't drive home like this. I'm sopping wet."

"Of course, come with me," Paul's mother said, leading the way.

The two women were only gone a few minutes when Paul heard shrieking from inside the house. He and his father rushed inside to see Vicky holding her hand out, fingers splayed. "Oh no, oh no," she wailed, completely distraught. "Oh no, Leah. This is terrible."

Paul's mother was silent, but the color had drained from her face. Paul thought maybe someone had died.

"What's wrong?" Dad asked.

"Somehow I've lost Leah's beautiful ring," Vicky said. "I have no idea how it happened, truly. I had it on my finger the last time I looked."

Dad held up a hand. "It couldn't have gone far. You had it on your finger when you fell into the pool, right?"

Vicky nodded.

"Then it has to be somewhere in the pool area."

The group trooped back outside to look. Paul dove into the water and searched the floor of the pool. He held his breath as long as he could, and he went down several times, but Paul still couldn't find the ring. The adults looked in the area surrounding the pool and even farther back in the backyard, thinking that maybe it flew off her hand when she fell backward. They finally admitted defeat an hour later.

"It's just gone," Mom said, sinking onto a patio chair in resignation. "My beautiful ring—and I only had it for a day."

Aunt Vicky said, "Leah, I can't tell you how sorry I am." She did sound sorry, not that it helped.

"I'll live," Mom said glumly. "Don't worry about it."

"Tell you what," Vicky said. "Let's go shopping next weekend, and I'll buy you a replacement. We can go to the jewelry store up on Idlewild Drive, and you can pick out anything you want. They have some beautiful things."

Paul waited for his mother to explode in anger. That would have been her response normally, but not this time. Miracle of miracles, she said, "Oh, you don't have to do that, Vicky. I know it's not your fault."

"Please let me," Vicky said. "It would be a favor to me because it would make me feel better."

"If you insist," Mom said, straightening up in her chair. "It's not really necessary, but if it would make you feel better, I'll do it for you."

"It might still turn up," Dad said. "Sometimes things like that happen." But neither of the women looked convinced.

CHAPTER FIFTEEN

*L*ater that evening, Mom let Clem out to do his business. She left the dog sniffing around in the grass and went back in to watch TV. "Dumb dog doesn't know what he wants," she said to Paul's dad. "One minute he's barking at the door like it's an emergency, and when he finally gets out he wanders around like a tourist taking in the sights."

"Oh, leave him be," Dad said. "He'll let us know when he wants to come back in."

Outside, Clem circled around the pool, trying to figure out what he was supposed to do. He had the strangest urges lately. He'd always been protective of Paul, so of course he watched out for him. Lately, though, his instincts were more specific. When that boy Henry came out of the woods last week, Clem somehow knew he was bad news and that he had to sound the alarm. And now he knew to search for the lost ring. He followed his nose, somehow sensing it was at the bottom of the pool. No turning back now. If he wanted to get it, he'd have to go in the water.

He leaped in, joyfully. Clem loved swimming, but he knew that Paul's mother wouldn't like him in the pool. He'd gotten in trouble once already for going in when he was alone in the backyard. He looked at the window, but no one was there. He might get away with it this time.

He doggy-paddled in circles, periodically looking down to check. Finally he spotted something below on top of the filter drain. It looked metallic, but he wasn't entirely sure it was the ring. Only one way to find out.

In he dove, forcing his way down to the bottom and coming up with the ring in his mouth. He scrambled out of the pool, the ring clenched between his teeth, shook off hard, and rolled around on the grass to dry off. Paul's mother was going to be angry if he was wet when she opened the door.

Lucky for Clem, the one who opened the door was Paul. "Hey there, Clem," he said. "Come on in." And then he noticed that the dog's fur was damp and matted down. "Why are you all wet, boy?"

The words coming out of Clem's mouth were a little garbled because of the ring, but he answered, "I was in the pool."

"What?" Paul's mouth dropped open, and his eyes widened in shock.

Clem dropped the ring at Paul's feet. "Don't tell your mom, but I was in the pool." He panted heavily. "Was looking for the ring, and I found it. Here ya go."

Paul jumped from foot to foot, something he did when he was excited. "Clem, you can talk." He leaned down to look into the dog's eyes. "I can't believe you can talk."

"I've always talked," Clem said, shaking his body to get rid of the excess moisture. "No one understood me, though."

"Boy oh boy," Paul said, slapping his thigh. "This is unbelievable. Wait until I tell Alex and Celia. Totally weird and amazing. You could be like a totally famous dog. I'll be famous. I'll be the kid who has the talking dog. Unreal." He ran his hand through his hair and thought of all the possibilities. His family would be rich. What would they do with all the money? A trip to Disney World for sure, and who knew what else.

"Come with me," Paul said, pulling on Clem's collar. This was too good to keep to himself. His parents were going to fall over when they heard the dog talking.

CHAPTER SIXTEEN

Clem stiffened his legs and resisted being pulled. For the first time ever, he could voice an objection. "Where we going?" he sputtered.

Paul paused and grinned. This really was happening. "We have to show my parents you can talk. They're going to be amazed." This was especially true for Paul's mother, who thought the dog was an unnecessary expense. When she'd found a mouse in the basement, she'd dragged Clem downstairs, but the dog had no interest in catching it. If anything, he looked a little scared. "We should trade this dog in for a cat," she'd said at the time. Now that Clem could talk, she'd see how wrong she'd been.

"I'm not talking to *them*," Clem said, sitting his back end firmly on the tile floor.

"Why not?" Paul asked, flabbergasted.

"I don't care what they think. You talk to me all the time. You're the only one I ever wanted to talk to." Clem cocked his head to one side. "You ask me questions. I've wanted to answer, but I couldn't. Think of all the fun we can have now!" He leaned forward and licked Paul's hand.

"So you won't talk to my parents?" Paul said.

"Nope."

"Not even a few words? For me? Please?"

"Uh-uh, no way, no how," Clem said. "They'll just make a big fuss about it. I want my peace and quiet. I don't wanna do tricks for people. What a pain."

Paul knew the feeling. It was like when he first learned his multiplication tables and his mother wanted him to show his grandmother. "Paul, show Grandma that you know your times tables. What's nine times nine?" He'd answered, "Eighty-one," and both his mother and grandmother had applauded. How annoying.

His mother would have gone on and on quizzing him except his father had stopped it, saying, "He's not a trained monkey, Leah. Give the kid a break."

Still, having a dog talk was a different thing altogether. "I'll give you your favorite treat," Paul said. "Anything you want?"

Clem's ears perked up. "Anything?"

"Anything. And as much as you want."

The dog thought hard. Paul had always imagined that this particular expression was Clem's thoughtful look, and now he knew for sure this was true. A minute later, Clem shook his head. "Nah. Don't wanna. Thanks anyways."

Paul sighed. He knew how stubborn Clem could be. "Just think about it for a while. You might change your mind."

"Doubtful," Clem said.

"How is it you can talk, anyway?" Paul asked. "You never did before."

"It's the ring," Clem said. "It's a magic thing."

"How do you know that?" Paul said.

"We better go to your room to talk," Clem said. "It's a long story."

From the next room Paul's mom called out, "Paul, who are you talking to? Who's there?"

Clem shook his head, warning him not to tell.

Paul said, "No one's here, Mom. I'm just talking to Clem."

CHAPTER SEVENTEEN

*B*ack in the woods, Mira and Jasmine settled against the base of a tree to talk. The weather was hot, but it was cool in the shade, and they could always use their wings to generate a slight breeze if need be.

"How is it that you know all about the ring?" Jasmine asked.

Mira arranged her skirt around her knees. "This goes back a long way, to when I was the fairy responsible for Celia's house."

"Celia, you mean Paul's friend?"

"No, the original Celia, her grandmother."

Jasmine looked confused, so Mira clarified. "They both have the same name. The little girl was named after her grandmother. Back when I was in charge of the house, there was only one Celia, and that was the original Celia. Now she's an old lady, but back in the day she was a lively little thing."

Jasmine stared in fascination. "How long ago was this?"

"Sixty years or so. There were two girls back then, Celia and her sister Josie," Mira said.

"And the ring belonged to one of them?"

Mira playfully shook a finger at her. "You're getting ahead of me, missy. Let me tell it."

"Okay," Jasmine said.

"It was Celia and Josie in one house, and in the other house, the one where Paul lives, there was a boy named Silas McClutchy."

"Paul's grandfather?"

"Now you're getting it," Mira said.

A slight breeze brought the scent of pine to them, a clean smell, Jasmine thought. She said, "So the ring belonged to Silas McClutchy?"

"No," Mira said. "The ring didn't belong to anyone. It's actually not a nice ring at all even though it gives the wearer a wish, the one wish they've always wanted. Not a wish that gives you a thing, but one that gives an ability, a talent, see? And not just any talent like playing the piano or singing, but a superhuman ability. Above and beyond what's normal."

"I don't get it," Jasmine said. "So this ring just showed up one day? It had to belong to someone."

Mira sighed. "I'm not sure where it came from originally, but it was Silas who found it, and he showed it to his friend Henry. There was some kind of fight between them, and Henry wound up taking the ring. And he got more than he bargained for because the one thing he always wanted was to never grow up, and that's exactly what he got."

"What did he get?" Jasmine asked.

"He never got any older from the day he first put on the ring."

Jasmine gasped. "He's been the same age for sixty years?"

Mira nodded. "Never aged, not even a day. His parents took him to doctors to find out why he wasn't getting taller. Eventually all the kids his age got deeper voices and started to grow whiskers, but not Henry. He was doomed. Eventually his family moved to Europe. I heard that they were looking for a cure in Switzerland. So many years ago." She stared off in the distance and shook her head. "Back then, the fairy in charge of Henry's family arranged to have the ring thrown into a well so it couldn't damage anyone else's life. Eventually that well dried up and was filled in. The ring might have stayed underground forever if Paul hadn't found it when they were digging for the pool. I often wondered what happened to Henry, and now he's turned up. I would imagine he's outlived everyone in his family."

"How horrible. Couldn't he unwish it?"

"Nope, once it's done, it's done. That's the problem with the ring and why it's so awful. People think they want these outlandish things, but once they get them, it's really a curse."

"And *that's* why Vicky McClutchy can swim now," Jasmine said. "That was her wish." She tapped her chin thoughtfully. "But that doesn't make sense because swimming isn't a superhuman talent."

Mira said, "It is for Vicky. She was traumatized as a child and was terrified of water."

"So her wish is a good thing."

"The wishes always seem good at the start, but wait, it gets worse."

"So what do I do about it?" Jasmine asked. Her job was to safeguard Paul and his parents, but how could she do that when there was a chance the ring might do its evil magic?

"You have to get control of the ring," Mira said. "It's the only way. Obviously, burying it didn't work. You'll need to destroy it completely this time."

Jasmine shuddered. She didn't know how she could do that; her power was so limited. Fairies couldn't risk being seen by people, and they couldn't make human beings do anything. All they could do was offer suggestions and guidance. "How would I destroy it?"

"Heck if I know. Everyone else up to now has failed. But you're a smart girl. I'm sure you'll think of something." Mira patted her arm. "Well, I have a lot of work to do, so if you don't have any more questions, I think I'll be off." She got to her feet and fluttered away, leaving Jasmine twisting her hands in despair.

CHAPTER EIGHTEEN

O nce they were in Paul's bedroom, Clem explained about the magic ring. "Yup. It gives people the gift they want the most," he said and then stopped to sniff around on the carpeting. "Something supernatural. Like how I got to talk."

"So it was the magic of the ring that made you talk?" Paul asked incredulously.

"Sure as can be. I had the ring in my mouth, and I was just wishin' I could talk, and then I could," Clem said. He licked at the carpeting and then looked up at Paul. "You musta spilled something in here once. Tastes like apple juice."

"That was a long time ago," Paul said. "Like months ago."

"I can still smell it," Clem said happily, "and taste it too."

Paul pulled the ring out of his pocket. "So how do you know about the ring's magic?"

Clem shifted his front paws. "I just know. Ideas come into my head sometimes. Dogs are kind of psychic, ya know."

How fascinating. Paul had always suspected that Clem had the inside track on things, but he could never prove it. His mother thought the dog was dumb. And lazy. Well, she was half right, but oh boy, was she wrong about the other half! He suddenly thought of a way he could show the world that Clem could talk. He would borrow his dad's camera…

"Don't even think about recording me talking," Clem said, settling down for a snooze. "I'll know if you're doing it, and I won't talk. No way, no how."

"How did you know that's what I was thinking?" Paul asked.

"Told ya. Dogs are psychic."

"Oh."

"Now I'm gonna go to sleep. Totally exhausted." Clem's eyes closed, and he put one paw over his nose, his favorite napping position.

Paul put the ring on his finger and tried to think of other things to wish for, but nothing came readily to mind. He considered a few options: Being six feet tall? Being so smart he got all As? Running faster than any other kid in his class? None of them really hit the mark for him, and he realized there wasn't any one thing he'd always wanted. Maybe for Brody at school to leave him alone and stop calling him Spaz, but that wasn't really a gift.

He'd have to think on this some more. In the meantime, he couldn't let his mother see the ring. She'd want it back and would probably waste her wish on something lame. No, it was better if he had it.

CHAPTER NINETEEN

*H*enry noticed Aunt Vicky had the ring on her finger the day of the party, and he also saw that it was gone when she emerged from the pool. Logically, he knew it must have come off while she was swimming. She was in the water a long time. A ring could slide off so easily.

Hours after the pool party was over, when he knew Clem was in the house and the rest of the family was busy, he stripped down to his skivvies and dove into the pool to search for it. No luck, although there was one bonus: the chlorinated water gave him a much-needed bath.

After that, he hid in the woods watching and waiting. The ring had to turn up eventually, and when it did, Henry was going to get it no matter what it took. He needed that ring. He had to have it. It was the only way he could fix a lifetime of misery.

Henry knew that he couldn't unwish his wish because what was done was done, but maybe he could make a new wish, one that involved going back in time. He'd just come up with that idea, and it was a good one. Yes, that's what he'd do—he'd wish he could time travel. Then he'd go back in time and warn his younger self. He'd tell his younger self not to go near the ring and not to even think about how nice it would be to never grow up. That was the only way.

On Sunday, the day after the pool party, he was perched up in a tree when Paul came walking into the woods, Clem at his side. At the sight of the dog, Henry stiffened in alarm. He was deathly afraid of dogs, and Clem was big even if he was old and slow. Henry listened curiously as Paul paused to talk to Clem.

"I still haven't decided what I'm going to wish for," Paul said. "I've been thinking it would be cool to run really fast or maybe be incredibly strong or something."

Henry drew in a sharp breath. It sounded like Paul had found the ring, knew about the magic, and was actually going to wish for something. This was very bad. Someone should warn him the ring had dark powers—someone should tell him that wishing would be a terrible mistake. He opened his mouth to call and get his attention, but just then something shocking happened: the dog talked!

"Those are kind of dopey wishes," the dog said, yawning. "Now, a talking dog, that's something worthwhile."

"I'm starting to wish you didn't talk," Paul said. "You kept waking me up last night when I was trying to sleep."

"Yup, yup. I kept thinking of stuff to tell ya."

"All of it could have waited." Paul reached down and picked up a stick. He threw it as if to play fetch, but Clem didn't budge. "All you talked about was how things smell and that you didn't like the new water dish."

"All important stuff to say," Clem said. "Yup, I gotta say things now that I can."

"Sure, you can go and on about stupid things like that, but you won't talk to my parents," Paul said bitterly.

Up in the tree, Henry listened in fascination. How long had the dog been talking? And how? It's not like he could wear the ring. The dog kept yammering on about nothing in particular, and Paul grumbled back at him. As they wandered off, Henry hatched a new plan to get the ring back.

CHAPTER TWENTY

*T*he next day, when Paul was invited to play at his friend Alex's house, he tucked the ring into his pocket. At some point he planned on showing it to his friend and telling him everything that had happened since he'd discovered it in the hole.

Alex always wanted to come to Paul's house because he thought playing in the woods was fun, but Paul thought Alex had the better end of the deal. His house was in a sub-division called Crescent Cover, and Alex's house was in the middle of a big cul-de-sac. All the kids in the area gathered in the street in front of Alex's house with their skateboards. Alex's dad had built a ramp for them. If a kid got up enough speed, he could get some real lift going. It drove the moms crazy, but the boys loved it. When Paul's mother dropped him off, she'd slowed to avoid all the kids who were skate-boarding and biking in front of Alex's house. "I certainly wouldn't like this," she said, her mouth turning downward. "I worry about someone getting hurt."

"Everyone's real careful, Mom," Paul said, although it was clear that wasn't true. One boy, in fact, had his arm in a cast supported by a neon green sling.

"None of them are wearing helmets, either. That's not good." She rolled down her window as she pulled into Alex's driveway, and for a minute Paul was afraid that she was going to yell something to the kids. How mortifying. She didn't though, just gave him a pat and said, "I'll be back at four to pick you up." She was getting better, Paul thought as he got out of the car. She used to insist on walking him up to the door and talking to the mom of the house. Yes, things were much better now than they used to be.

Alex was already outside, and he waved Paul over to where the boys were skateboarding. "Hey, Paul! Over here."

Two girls riding scooters circled around the boys and laughed. Paul knew they were a grade older than him, same as Celia, but these were silly girls, the kind who shrieked and laughed about nothing. They were such a pain. Why did they hang around?

Paul didn't own a skateboard because his mom didn't approve. All of the other boys were better than him. Even the smaller ones could do kickflips and spins, maneuvers he couldn't manage. It made him feel like an idiot, so he was glad when Alex's mom walked out from the house and told them to put the ramp away. "One of the neighbors is complaining about the noise," she said. "Let's just call it a day. You boys can do something else." She suddenly noticed Paul. "Oh hi, Paul. When did you get here?" Alex's mom was lackadaisical and didn't really keep track of things. Paul liked that quality in a parent.

"I've been here for a while," he said. Something about her friendly manner spurred him to add a polite, "Thanks for letting me come over today."

"What good manners," she said. "You're very welcome, Paul."

She went back inside, and the rest of the neighbor kids wandered off, the fun interrupted. Paul dragged the ramp into the garage. Alex put his skateboard away and then went inside to get some cold Cokes. Another thing Paul's mom wouldn't have approved of. She said Paul was naturally caffeinated, the way he bounced around all the time.

When Alex came out with the drinks, the boys went to the backyard. There weren't many trees there, but there was a play structure Alex's dad had built. A big wooden thing with two slides, a climbing rope, and a covered platform, which Alex called "the tree house." Truthfully, this was better for younger kids, but it was still good for them to have a place to go. And they were in the shade, which was a bonus.

"I asked my mom if we could come in and play video games, and she said absolutely not, that it's a beautiful day and we should stay outside." Alex made a face before sipping from his can of Coke.

"It's okay," Paul said. "This is good."

"Maybe when the baby gets up from his nap, she'll let us in," Alex said.

Paul dug into his pocket. "I've got something kind of cool to show you." He pulled out the ring. "Look at this. I found it in a treasure chest that was buried underground. It was uncovered when the workers were digging out the pool."

"No way!" Alex said. "What was it doing there?"

"I don't know," Paul said. "I was just looking down in the hole one night after the crew left, and I saw a square thing sticking out of the dirt. I got my dad's ladder and climbed down and dug it out."

"Hand it over. I want to see it." Alex reached out, and Paul reluctantly put it in his palm.

"Is this the ring your mom had at the pool party?"

Paul hesitated. "Yeah, I let her wear it for a while." It was too complicated to explain.

Alex gave it a careful looking over. "Looks like something a knight would wear. Cool."

"Be careful. I think it's worth a lot of money."

"I'm surprised your mom lets you carry it around," Alex said. Paul's mom was known for being persnickety.

Paul said, "She doesn't know I have it."

"Whoa!" Alex gave Paul an approving look. "Good for you."

Paul wanted to tell him that the ring was magic. Alex was his best friend and would certainly keep the secret. Paul was also dying to tell him that the ring was what made his Aunt Vicky into a swimmer, and that now, believe it or not, Clem could talk. He hoped Alex would believe him. Paul took a sip from his drink. "You won't believe this, Alex, but the ring—"

Before he could get the words out, a yell from down below interrupted him. A loud, raucous yell. "Hey, Alex, where are you?"

Alex leaned over the side of the platform. "Up here," he said.

When Paul saw who it was, his heart sank. It was Brody, the bully. Paul thought he'd get a break during summer vacation, but here he was, his mortal enemy, looking as terrifying as he'd remembered. "What's he doing here?" Paul asked.

"He moved in down the block last week," Alex said. "He's okay, really he is, Paul. It's cool."

Brody came up to join them, his footsteps heavy on the wooden ladder. "Dude, whatcha doing?" His eyes caught on Paul, and he sneered disdainfully. "Hey, why is Spaz here?"

"He wanted to come over," Alex said, rolling his eyes, "and my mom said it was okay." Paul could tell from Alex's tone that he'd switched alliances. A minute before they'd been good friends, but now that Brody was here, Paul was the outsider.

Brody scrambled up and took a seat, his massive bottom filling up a third of the platform. "So what's going on?"

"Paul found this cool ring digging in his backyard like one of those scientist guys that looks for fossils." Alex held out the ring, and Brody reached for it.

Oh no. Paul's heart slammed against his ribcage, and he leaped forward to grab it, but it was too late.

"Not so fast there, Spaz," Brody said. "Let me see what you got."

CHAPTER TWENTY-ONE

"Give that to me," Paul yelled, reaching for the ring.

But Brody had a firm grip on it. He held it above his head, out of Paul's reach. "Easy there, Spaz, I'm not going to ruin your precious jewelry. I just want to take a look at it."

"It's mine," Paul said, blinking hard to fight back tears. Crying would be the worst thing in the world. Knowing what a blabbermouth Brody was, he'd tell everyone at school and Paul would never hear the end of it.

Brody stood up and put the ring on his thumb. "I like it." He pushed Paul away. "Good job digging it up for me, little guy. Nice of you."

"No," Paul said. "Give it back. It belongs to me. My mom will be so mad if I don't bring it home."

Brody shrugged. "So you're going to tell on me?" He curled his hand into a fist and gestured to Alex. "Why are you hanging out with this loser, Al?"

Alex looked uncomfortable. "Give him back his ring, Brody. You're going to get in trouble."

"Says who?" Brody took the ring off and waved it in front of Paul's face. "Take a good look, you big baby, this is the last you'll see of your ring. Or should I say, *my* ring."

Paul had tears in his eyes now, but he didn't wipe them away. Instead, he threw himself at Brody's outstretched arm, knocking Brody off balance. The ring flew up in the air, Brody fell backwards onto his butt, and Paul, catching hold of the ring, found himself catapulting off the platform and plummeting down to the earth. He saw the ground coming up at him, and just one millimeter from hitting the ground, a stray thought hit his brain. *I wish I could fly.*

CHAPTER TWENTY-TWO

*R*ight before Paul hit the dirt, his wish took hold and he found himself up in the air soaring over Alex and Brody.

"What the…" Brody said. Paul didn't catch the rest because he'd already flown out of hearing distance. Whoa! So this is what it felt like to fly. Birds were so lucky. They got to do this all the time, and now he could do it too. His heart pounded happily, and he discovered he could control his movement by flexing his body and flapping his arms. It was a lot like swimming, but it took less effort. So cool.

He glanced downward and saw Alex and Brody looking up at him, shocked and awed. On the earth below, his boy-shaped shadow moved quickly and changed shape as he twisted and turned. This was too awesome for words. He thought of how inept he was on the skateboard and realized it didn't matter anymore. He might be a total loser on wheels, but he was probably the only kid in the world who could fly. Really, there was no comparison. He ruled.

He heard the two boys down below calling his name. "Come down," Alex yelled, waving frantically. It was hard to

see at this height, but it almost looked like Alex and Brody were afraid. Their faces were scrunched, and they each held a hand over their forehead to shield their eyes from the sun. What were they worried about? Paul had never felt better.

"Woo hoo!" he called out, swooping down and back up again in an elegant arc. He was really getting the hang of this.

Brody waved both hands like trying to signal a rescue ship off in the distance. Paul ignored him, but the sight of Brody reminded him that he still had the ring clenched in his hand. Still airborne, he slid the ring on his middle finger and found it to be a nice fit. The ring wasn't going anywhere.

"Come back," Alex shouted, but Paul wasn't about to stop. He wanted to fly forever.

He dove in closer, and both Alex and Brody ducked like they were being attacked. "I'm going home now, Alex," he yelled down. "Tell your mom thanks for the Coke." He didn't wait for a response, just took off. He knew it was bad manners to leave like that, but Alex had Brody to hang out with, so he probably wouldn't miss Paul at all. Alex seemed to think Brody was cooler than Paul, but that was before Paul took to the air. He'd really showed them. Ha!

A few blocks away, Paul heard the sounds of a jet above him. He hovered and waved, but the jet was so high and going so fast he doubted they saw him. Too bad. He rose upward until the houses were the size of Monopoly pieces. It was windier up high, so he came back down. He was still getting the hang of this, but the right height seemed to be just above the tree line and telephone wires. On the sidewalk below him, a woman pushed a stroller holding a baby boy. The little guy wore a red baseball cap and a pair of oversized sunglasses. He had two fingers stuck in his mouth and drooled. As Paul flew overhead, the child pointed and said something that sounded like, "Garby ooluf."

"Yes, yes, honey," said his mother. "We'll be home very soon."

Paul headed in the direction of his house. He'd never realized how the town was laid out before. From this new vantage point, he noticed how many people had pools. And look at all the cars driving around during the day! Where were they all going? He flew over the industrial park and saw men emptying trucks at the loading docks. How odd that no one noticed a boy flying overheard. People were so short-sighted. They only seemed to see what was ahead of them. "Hello," he yelled, but no one even looked up.

He was getting tired now and decided to go straight home. If Celia was out in her yard, he could fly right over her. Wouldn't that blow her mind! The sun was starting to feel intense on his back, and he considered flipping over to see if he could fly that way, but if it worked, he wouldn't be able to see where he was going. With his luck, he'd fly right into a pole or tree or something. No, he'd just keep going the way he was.

When he got closer to home, the woods got thicker. From up here the trees looked like clusters of broccoli, so green and thick. When he flew nearer, he could see the individual branches and leaves, but he didn't want to look down for too long. The motion made him a little sick.

He reached Celia's house, but she wasn't outside. Too bad. He considered landing and knocking at the door, but he was sweaty and tired and just wanted to go home. Maybe he would go for a swim, and afterward he could show Celia his new talent. Perhaps he'd start off by saying they should pretend to fly by jumping out of trees. They'd done this before, so she wouldn't think too much about it, he thought. He'd leap a few times, and then, when she wasn't expecting it, he'd levitate just a little bit. She'd be amazed, of course, and from there he'd work his way up to flying above her head. He laughed out loud just thinking about how she was gonna flip out.

Yes, that's what he'd do. He knew Celia would be happy for him. She was a true friend, he saw that now. She almost always agreed to let him play what he wanted to play, which made her pretty fun to be around. He wanted to show her how Clem could talk too. He knew Clem didn't want to talk to the grown-ups, but hopefully he'd make an exception for Celia, who always rubbed behind his ears and talked so sweetly to him even during the times Paul had thought Clem was being a pest.

He did a perfect landing in his backyard, setting down as lightly as if he'd been flying for years. Clem came trotting around from the side of the house, his mouth hanging open. "Hey, Paul," he said.

Paul just now noticed that Clem's voice had an annoying nasal quality. Before he'd been so amazed that Clem could talk that he hadn't thought too much about it. "Hey, Clem, guess what? I can fly."

"Okay," Clem said and snarfed. "Know what, Paul? I saw grasshoppers, and one of them went really high. Yup. Really, really high. They push off with their legs, ya know. I caught one and ate it. It was kind of crunchy."

Paul leaned over, putting his hands on his knees. "You know you shouldn't eat insects. That's disgusting."

"No, not disgusting," Clem said. "Crunchy I tell ya, and it squirted a little in my mouth."

Talking to Clem was such an unsatisfying experience. Half the time, the dog didn't even listen. Once more Paul tried telling him his big news. "Hey guess what, Clem?" he said. Not waiting for a reply, he continued, "I can fly now. I had the ring in my hand, and I made a wish, and that's what I wished for. You should have seen me. I was soaring over houses and zooming above trees. It was awesome."

He didn't get the desired reaction. Clem said, "Yup. I know the feeling. One time I jumped really high and my ears kind of went up and my fur went fluffy for a second. I was like a duck. Yup, like a duck. I know that flying feeling."

"That's not the same at all," Paul said. "I was actually flying. Look," he said, shaking his hands and rising a foot above the ground. He dropped back down and said, "If I wasn't so tired, I'd show you. I can fly, really fly. Like a plane, or a helicopter, or a bird. I can do something no one else can. I was over at Alex's house, and that nasty Brody was there giving me a hard time. I stood right up to him even though he's bigger than me. I said, 'Give me back my ring!' and I knocked him down and grabbed it from him, and I must have been thinking the wish because the next thing I knew I was lighter than air. Brody was sorry he'd been so mean to me. He got down on his knees and begged my forgiveness." Okay, it wasn't the complete truth, but he'd only changed the story slightly. Most of it was the same. Ninety-five percent anyway.

"I need more water in my water dish," Clem said, looking around. And he took off, barking.

Paul sighed. Talking dogs were so annoying.

The back door opened, and his mother stuck her head out. "Oh, there you are." She had the phone pressed against her ear. "Don't worry, he's here now." She glared in Paul's direction. "No, don't worry about it. I'm glad you called. Yes, I've got it from here. Thanks. Bye." She closed the phone and beckoned with one finger. "Come inside right now, young man. That was Alex's mom on the phone. You've got some explaining to do."

CHAPTER TWENTY-THREE

*A*s always, Jasmine was taking care of business. She had been perched on the branch of a tree watching the house when she saw Paul come flying home, his face flushed and red. This whole thing was

getting out of hand. She was horrified. She found herself wishing she was in charge of the old retired man on the corner. That guy's biggest problem was losing the remote.

"What to do, what to do?" she said to herself. She flapped her wings to create a breeze. Maybe some cool air would help her think.

Was there no end to the complications at Paul's house? First there was a magic ring, which needed to be destroyed. Secondly, was there anything more annoying than a talking dog? She didn't think so. All that talk of water dishes and how things smelled was getting to be tiresome. Aunt Vicky turning into a swimmer didn't seem to be such a big deal, although Mira had indicated it would get to be a problem. And now the boy, Paul, could fly. Great, just great. She tapped her toe against a rock and thought hard. Worst-case scenario, the kid would fly into a power line and electrocute himself. If that happened, she'd definitely get demoted. Oh why did she get assigned the difficult house?

She furrowed her brow and concentrated on what was happening inside with Paul and his mother. In her mind's eye she could see that Paul was getting a good talking to, that his mother was saying something about how he shouldn't have walked home on his own, that it was dangerous and he could have gotten killed. By tuning into their thought waves, she could hear their conversation as well. "I love you so much," his mother said, pulling him into a hug that left him breathless and unable to talk. "I wouldn't have been able to bear it if anything had happened to you."

Jasmine could tell that he wanted to tell her about the flying, but he couldn't get a word in edgewise.

His mother kept a firm hold on Paul. "Alex's mother was so concerned about you. Alex came in babbling something about you flying away. He was white as a ghost and said he needed to take a nap. He's never been like that before, according to his mother. She wanted to know if that Brody was bothering you boys. He's got quite a reputation for meanness, she said. Was he bothering you? You can tell me if he was."

Paul swallowed and shook his head.

"Are you sure? He wasn't harassing you?"

"No, Mom, Brody was fine." He smiled at the thought of Brody's open mouth when Paul zoomed past.

"Well, okay then, but if anyone ever bullies you, I want you to know you can tell your father and me." And then the doorbell rang, and Paul's mother was distracted. "Go to your room and think about what I said about walking home without permission," she told Paul. "I'll go see who that is."

CHAPTER TWENTY-FOUR

*P*aul's mom opened the front door to find her sister Vicky standing on the welcome mat. Vicky wore a turquoise one-piece swimming suit with a towel wrapped around her middle. On her head was a stretchy tan bathing cap. It completely covered her hair, giving her a bald look. "Hi, sis," she bellowed. "Glad to see me?"

Paul's mom couldn't hold back her surprise. "Vicky, what's going on?"

"I came to go swimming. I'm finding that I can't think of anything else lately. I was in the middle of a board meeting at my company. We were discussion a new division that would cost a few million dollars, and I couldn't concentrate. All I could think about was how good the water feels when I'm floating on my back. Well, let me tell you, I told them to do whatever they thought was best, and I left the meeting."

"You left work to swim?" Paul's mother asked incredulously.

"You don't mind, do you?" Vicky pointed to the towel around her waist. "I brought everything I need, and you

don't need to stop what you're doing. Just go about your business as if I wasn't even here."

"Oh, okay, I guess."

Vicky stepped inside and walked through the house toward the patio door with Paul's mom following her. "If Paul wants to join me, tell him I'd love the company," she said, sliding open the door. "I'll be swimming for hours."

Paul's mom watched her for a few minutes through the patio door. This was so unlike Vicky. But of course, her sister *had* changed a lot lately. She tried to think of how to describe Vicky now and only came up with one word. Nice. Vicky was nice. No more mean looks or snarky comments. No more telling Paul to "get lost." Vicky was nice now. What a refreshing change.

It was odd, but wonderful. Clem came up alongside Paul's mom, and she rested her hand on his head. "Hi, boy," she said. "Will you take a look at Vicky out there? Nicer than she's ever been, and swimming when she's always been afraid of the water. Have you ever seen anything so amazing in your life?" Clem whined quietly, and she rubbed behind his ears. "No, I haven't either."

CHAPTER TWENTY-FIVE

*H*enry watched from his perch on a tree limb as Aunt Vicky came out of the house. She dropped the towel on the patio and slipped gracefully into the pool. Once in, she floated happily on her back, kicking occasionally, causing little ripples of water. Her face showed complete contentment.

From Henry's vantage point there was a clear view into Paul's second story bedroom, and he could see the boy walking around. Henry had seen Paul flying home earlier and knew, without a doubt, that the ring was responsible for this new development. He also noticed the ring on Paul's hand. At least he knew where it was now.

Henry had spent the last several days brainstorming ways to get the ring back. His ideas covered everything from sneaking into the house (not possible since he was afraid of the dog), to luring Paul out into the woods, then knocking him down and taking it by force (too risky). Just when he'd run out of notions, something unexpectedly came to him. The idea popped into his mind in a clearly spoken voice, almost as if someone else had planted the idea. The voice said: *Ask Paul for the ring. Explain what happened and just ask. He'll understand and hand it over.*

At first he dismissed the thought. It seemed like it wouldn't work, but the voice in his mind was insistent. *Paul is a good boy*, the voice said. *He'll do it.*

What was he waiting for? Now was as good a time as ever. Henry shimmied down the tree, took a deep breath and stealthily made his way around the house, avoiding the pool area. Paul's room was in the corner, with one window facing the backyard and one on the side. Henry slowly tiptoed underneath the side window, cupped his hands around his mouth, and whispered loudly, "Paul." No response.

Henry tried again. "Paul!"

This time he was heard. Paul came to the window, startled to see Henry staring up at him. "Yes?" he said.

CHAPTER TWENTY-SIX

*P*aul had been sitting on his bed, flipping through comic books when he heard someone call his name. He was shocked to see it was that boy, the one Celia's grandma said looked like someone she knew from a long time ago. "What do you want?" he asked. He rested his hands on the sill and leaned forward.

"Hello, Paul." The boy looked around nervously. "I'm Henry. I used to live in a house back in the woods." He pointed beyond the backyard. "I need a favor from you."

Paul suspected he was trying to pull something. There was no way Henry used to live in the woods. Everyone knew the woods was the shared property of the McClutchys and the Lovejoys, and had been since before Paul was born. "What house in the woods?" Paul asked. "I've never seen one."

Henry had a sudden look like he'd been caught in a lie. "It was a long time ago," he said. "My father used to work for your great-grandfather, and my family lived in the guesthouse."

"I have no idea what you're talking about," Paul said and tugged on the sash to close the window. It had a tendency to stick.

"No, don't do that," Henry said. "I can explain, please."

Paul knew his mother wouldn't approve of Henry being on their property, and she really wouldn't like it that Paul was talking to him. "You have to go," he said. "You don't belong here." He closed the window and reached up to turn the lock.

"I know about the ring." Henry's words came through the glass. "I know everything."

Paul undid the latch and pushed open the window. "What?"

"I know about the ring." Henry was talking quickly now. "I know it's magic. I had it once, a long time ago, and it got me into a big mess. I need to get it back to undo the spell I've been under for the last sixty-five years."

Paul hesitated. Sixty-five years? It sounded preposterous, but from the desperation in Henry's voice Paul sort of believed him. "What kind of spell are you talking about?"

A tear slid down Henry's face. "I've been stuck at this age for decades. Everyone in my family died, and I don't have any friends. I barely get enough to eat. I sleep wherever I can. I'm cold in the winter and hot in the summer. I wish I'd never found that ring."

Paul considered what Henry was saying. "I don't get it. What happened?"

"It's a long story," he said, brushing a strand of hair away from his face. "I stole the ring from my best friend, and I wished I'd never grow old. I thought it would be so wonderful to be young and live forever. I had no idea what was in store for me. My friend was smarter than me. He wished he would have the ability to make the world a better place. And he did. But for anyone who makes selfish wishes, it always backfires. That ring is evil."

Paul looked down at the ring on his finger. The polished gold and gemstone were so beautiful, it was hard to believe it was evil. "It didn't backfire for me," Paul said. "I can fly now, and let me tell you, it's amazing. I can dive through the air like nothing. It's the coolest thing ever."

"You say that now," Henry said bitterly. "Just wait. Something will go wrong—it always does."

The two were silent for a moment. Finally Paul said, "So what's the favor you want from me?"

"I need the ring back," Henry said. "So I can wish myself back in time and warn my younger self not to make the wish."

"No deal," Paul said. "I'm not giving the ring up to anyone. It's mine now, and that's the way it's going to stay."

Henry gestured frantically. "You can keep the ring. I don't even want it. I only need it for a minute to make my wish, and then you can have it back."

"You say that now," Paul said. "But I know how it goes. It'll be on your finger when you make the wish, and then you'll disappear and that will be the end of it. You'll be gone, and I'll never get the ring back."

"Please," Henry said. "I'm begging you. If there was another way I would do it, but there isn't. If you don't let me have the ring, I don't know what I'll do." His face scrunched up, and he wiped at his eyes with the back of his hand. "You have a mom and dad and a nice house—you can't possibly know what I'm going through." His voice was getting louder. "I'm begging you, Paul. Please. Show some compassion."

Paul sighed. "Let me think a minute." He tapped his fingers on the windowsill. It was one thing to know the right thing to do, another to have to do it. He looked at the ring again. If anything, it seemed to fit his finger even better, like it was made for him. It was so unfair to have to give it up when he was the one who found it.

"Please?" Henry pleaded. "I'd give you anything in the world, but I have nothing to give but my eternal gratitude."

"Okay, okay," Paul said. "You don't have to go on and on about it. I'll do it." He ran his hand over the window ledge. "I'd still be able to fly though, right?"

Henry nodded. "My wish wouldn't undo yours at all."

"Well in that case, I guess it will be okay." He started to take the ring off his finger when there was a knock on his bedroom door. "Just a minute, Mom, don't come in."

"Why not?" she asked from the other side.

Paul looked down at Henry and shrugged. Mothers could have such terrible timing. He turned to answer her. "Because I'm changing clothes. Just give me a sec."

Outside, by the pool, Clem started barking, making Henry visibly nervous. "I have to go now," Henry said. "I'll meet you in the woods tonight just as the sun is setting. You can give me the ring then. Don't bring the dog with you."

"Where in the woods?" Paul asked.

"There's a place straight back where three trees grow together like this." He put his hands together so his fingers intertwined.

Paul nodded. "I know it. My friend and I play there all the time."

"I'll meet you there."

Paul's mother called through the door, "Why are you changing anyway, in the middle of the day? I just wanted to let you know you can go swimming with Aunt Vicky if you want."

Paul said, "Okay, Mom." He turned back to the window to say good-bye to Henry, but the boy was already gone.

CHAPTER TWENTY-SEVEN

Jasmine stood up from the tree branch which over-looked Paul's yard and smoothed her skirt in a satisfied way. A good day's work and another problem solved. Yes, she was brilliant, if she said so herself.

She was the one who had put the idea in Henry's head to just ask Paul if he could have the ring. She should have thought of that in the first place. Why, nothing could be easier! Henry needed the ring; Paul already had his wish, so he really didn't need it anymore. It was a simple matter.

There were a few problems left behind, of course. The small issue of a talking dog, a flying boy, and an aunt with an obsession for swimming. Well, a fairy couldn't fix everything all in one day. She'd have to tackle these things soon, but at least she could cross Henry off her list. Oh, the joy of accomplishment. She fluttered her wings happily and pushed off so that she floated above the branch for just a second.

Below her, Henry ran back into the woods, looking fearfully behind him. He sure was afraid of the dog, which was

odd because Clem was more of a lovable furry rug than anything else. She shrugged. Who knew why people were the
way they were.

Jasmine was just about to lift off and head deeper into
the woods, when Mira startled her by landing silently at her
side. "Jasmine, my shining star," she said by way of a greet-
ing. "How are things going in the McClutchy house?"

Sensing that this was an official visit, Jasmine stood at
attention. "I'm happy to report that things are improving,"
she said. "Paul has agreed to give Henry the ring. Henry's
plan is to wish himself back in time so that he can warn his
younger self not to wish on the ring. A very good plan, I
believe. I gave him the idea myself." She smiled in satisfaction and waited for Mira to compliment her on her prob-
lem-solving skills. When that didn't happen, she continued.
"I know I still have to figure out what to do about Paul flying
and his aunt swimming, but I figured I'd tackle these issues
one at a time."

Mira harrumphed. "I think you've forgotten one other
problem—or do you think having a talking dog on the loose
won't attract attention?"

"No, Mira, I haven't forgotten. It's just that he hasn't
talked to anyone but Paul yet, so I feel that it's under control
for now." Jasmine was pleased that she was able to come up
with a reasonable response. How much trouble could Clem
be if he only talked to the boy?

"And how are you planning on dealing with all these
problems once the ring is gone?" Mira's eyes narrowed.
Jasmine knew that look and squirmed.

"I hadn't quite thought it through yet," she said.

"You hadn't quite thought it through yet?"

Jasmine suppressed the urge to ask if there was an echo in the woods. "No ma'am, but I'm still brainstorming different ideas. Since none of these problems is life-threatening, I figured I had time."

"You don't think a flying boy could potentially be life-threatening?" Mira's tone was definitely unfriendly now, maybe even a little angry. "The kid can't even walk across a room without bumping into something. How long do you think he can fly around without smashing into a building? The potential for disaster here is huge. Huge." Her eyes got big to illustrate.

Jasmine swallowed. This wasn't the reaction she was counting on. "I figured I had a little time, anyway."

"Not to mention," Mira said, "that Henry can't make another wish. The ring limits it to one wish per person."

"I didn't know that," Jasmine said. "And Henry and Paul don't seem to know that either, or I would have picked up on it."

"It was on the directions that came with the ring," Mira said. "Doesn't anyone read directions?" She threw up her hands in disgust.

"I guess not." Jasmine's eyes filled with tears. "So what should I do, Mira? When I asked you before, you said you were sure I'd figure something out. Now you say that what I want to do is no good. I could use some help here."

Mira sighed. "I do have a thought, but it's going to require a lot of work on your part."

"Just tell me what to do, and I'll do it."

CHAPTER TWENTY-EIGHT

*T*hat night, just as the sun was beginning to set, Paul slipped out the back door and headed toward the woods. He was nervous about leaving the house without permission. His parents were watching a show, but that would only hold them for a while and eventually they'd come looking for him. It would be good to get this over with quickly.

Henry had said not to bring the dog, and Paul was glad to comply. Clem's incessant talking was getting on his nerves. And the dog didn't have much of an attention span either. Paul had wanted to talk to someone about this ring business, but Clem wasn't the least bit helpful. Paul had poured out his heart out to Clem, saying that he'd promised to give the ring to Henry, but he still wasn't sure it was the right thing to do. "What do you think?" he'd asked.

"Magic rings are tricky things. Yup, tricky things," Clem said, shaking his head so hard his dog tags jangled. Then he got up off the rug and set off to look for his rawhide bone.

"Tricky things," Paul said aloud as he made his way past the tree line. He hoped Henry wouldn't keep him waiting for too long. He pushed past some bushes and kept going until he came to the small clearing in the middle of the three trees that he and Celia called the Triple Trees. "Henry," he called out, but there was no response. He wished he'd thought of bringing a flashlight. Shoot. Nervously he pushed off the ground and floated up a few feet. Levitating seemed to take more effort than actual flying, but he could manage it, and he was getting better with practice. At home he even managed to float above his bed for short periods of time.

The scampering of some small animal in the underbrush startled him so much that he dropped back down to earth. "Henry?" he said again, louder this time.

He glanced down at the ring on his finger and twisted it nervously. It was the coolest thing he ever owned, and now he was just handing it off to some kid he barely knew. If the story that Henry had been a kid for so long was true, then Paul was doing a good thing. It was hard to know the right thing to do.

Now he heard the sound of footsteps coming toward him. Quiet at first, and then louder, twigs snapping, branches being moved aside. It sounded too slow and heavy to be Henry.

Paul scrunched his forehead, wondering who it could be. Should he hide? No, he had every right to be here even if it was Lovejoy property. He and Celia played in this place all the time, and no one had ever objected.

He waited and listened until he heard a voice call out, "Paul?" An old lady, from the sound of it. And something about her voice sounded familiar. "Paul?" There it was again, and now he knew who it was: Celia's grandmother. What was she doing out in the dark at this time?

"Yes?" he answered, craning his neck to see.

Grammy came through the thicket of trees, carefully stepping over rocks and tree roots. She whispered, "I'm so glad I found you." She had a flashlight in her hand, and she clicked it on, aiming it toward the ground.

Paul waited for her to ask why he was out so late or to scold him for being on Lovejoy property, but she didn't do either. Instead, she pulled him into a hug. "I had a feeling you'd be here." She was whispering now. She released him from her grasp. "I take it that you're meeting Henry tonight."

Paul shook his head up and down. Words failed him for a minute. Finally he was able to ask, "How did you know?"

"Just a feeling, like I said. Do you mind if I wait here with you?" she asked. "Henry and I go way back, and I'd like to talk to him."

"He might get scared away if you're here," Paul said, looking around. He nervously twisted the ring around his finger.

"Oh, right," she said, and turned off the flashlight. "I'll hide in the bushes. When he gets here, I'll come out."

"How do you know Henry?" Paul asked, but Grammy was already heading out of the clearing.

Paul wondered if Henry would run off when Grammy came out of her hiding spot, but there wasn't much he could do about it. A thousand thoughts tumbled in his brain. Everything that had happened lately was bizarre; it all seemed like a dream. Everyone knew that dogs couldn't talk, and kids couldn't fly. Not unless they were in a plane, anyway. Or a helicopter. Or an ultra-light. Actually, there were more ways to fly than he'd realized, but flying without an aircraft was thought to be impossible. And yet, he could do it. Like a superhero.

A slight breeze came through the Triple Trees, making the branches sway. Paul knew Grammy was off to one side, watching and waiting too, and for some reason, that made him feel better. If something really horrible happened, he wasn't alone.

He'd almost decided Henry wasn't coming when he heard the same snap of twigs and rustling of underbrush he'd noticed when Grammy arrived. "Henry?" he whispered. "Is that you?"

"Yes." A voice came out of the darkness, and Henry came bursting between the trees. "It's me."

"I thought you weren't coming," Paul said.

"I lost track of time and fell asleep," Henry said, rubbing his eyes. "I'm glad you're still here. Did you bring the ring?"

"Yes, I have it." Paul twisted the ring on his finger.

"Hand it over," Henry said, "and I'll be on my way." His voice was tinged with excitement. "I can't wait to see my family again."

"Not so fast," Grammy said, entering the clearing. She turned on her flashlight. Paul blinked from the brightness. "I have to talk to you, Henry."

"You told," Henry said to Paul, accusingly. "This was supposed to be just between us. I trusted you."

Paul was insulted. "I didn't tell. I wouldn't do that. She just showed up."

"Paul didn't tell me," Grammy said, moving closer to the boys. She put her hand on Henry's shoulder, ready to grab him in the event he ran off. "I just got one of my feelings. You remember how I used to get those feelings, Henry?"

Henry looked puzzled. "Who are you?'

Grammy sighed. "I forgot that I must look completely different to you after all these years. I'm Celia. Remember me—Celia? We were once friends."

"Celia?" His eyes got wide. "But you look so old."

She laughed. "I am old, Henry. But I'm still the same person, and I think I can help you. I came up with a solution to your problem. Remember how ideas used to pop into my head like magic?"

"Messages from the fairies, you said. I made fun of you at the time."

"I wasn't supposed to tell anyone," she said. "I never should have said anything to you about it."

Paul looked at them in amazement. Fairies? What was all this?

"I didn't believe you," Henry said. "But now I know there are a lot of things out there that people never see. I'm sorry I laughed at you."

"And I'm sorry you never got a chance to grow up," she said sadly. "I've thought about you often over the years."

"It's not your fault," Henry said. "You tried to warn me. I just didn't listen."

"I don't understand," Paul said. "What's this about fairies?'

Grammy said, "That part isn't important. The main thing is fixing what the ring has done." She aimed her light on Paul's hand, illuminating the ring.

"I have it all worked out," Henry said. "Paul has agreed to hand over the ring. Once I have it in my possession, I'm going to wish that I can go back in time. Then I'll go back to before I made the wish and warn myself not to make the wish. It's a brilliant plan, if I do say so myself." He grinned. "I'll make sure to say hello to your younger self. Any words of advice you want me to give young Celia?"

Grammy shook her head sadly. "It is a brilliant plan. The only problem is that it won't work."

"Of course it will work," Henry said, indignant. "I've thought it through, and it'll work out perfectly. Why would you say such a thing?"

"It won't work," she said kindly, "because the ring only allows one wish per person. And you've already used up your wish."

Henry kicked at a pebble. "I never heard anything about only one wish."

"It's in the directions. Don't you remember?"

Paul thought back to the rolled-up piece of paper that came with the ring. Now that she mentioned it, he did remember a line that said something about "one use."

"She's right," Paul said. "Each person only gets one wish."

"I don't believe it," Henry said. "Both of you just want to keep me trapped here forever."

"Now why would we want to do that?" Grammy asked.

He pointed at Paul. "He just wants to keep the ring, and you're still upset with me from before when we argued."

"That was a long time ago," she said. "I'm not angry with you anymore. Believe me, I'd love to help fix your problem."

"I don't believe you." Henry spat out the words.

Grammy sighed. "There's only one way to convince him, Paul. Give him the ring and let him try."

Paul reluctantly pulled the ring off his finger and held it out. Henry eagerly took it.

"Yes," he said. "Oh, finally this will all be over and I can have a normal life again." Henry put the ring on his finger, closed his eyes, and said, "I wish I would go back in time to my house exactly four hours before I made the wish to never get older." He stood there with his eyes closed, and the three of them waited. Henry clicked his heels together and opened his eyes. "Why am I still here?" he asked, his voice anguished.

"I told you," Grammy said gently, "that it won't work. You already used up your turn."

"Then you do it," he said. "You wish it for me."

"I used up my wish too, remember?"

Paul listened to them talk and felt like an outsider. Hearing that Celia's grandmother made a wish on the ring a long time ago was definitely news. "What did you wish for?" he asked.

Grammy was silent for a minute, and then she said, slowly enunciating each word, "It was a long time ago. I'd rather not talk about it."

"She made a selfless wish," Henry said. "So it all turned out fine. It's just when you wish something for yourself that the whole thing goes bad."

"Maybe Paul can try making the wish for you," she suggested.

"He's used up his wish." Henry rolled his eyes. "He can fly."

"Oh my," Grammy said in a voice that suggested this was not a good thing.

"And not only that, but his dog can talk now," Henry said.

"Really," she said, turning to Paul. "It must be very interesting at your house nowadays."

Paul nodded. "So far there haven't been any real problems, though."

Henry cleared his throat. "And his aunt Vicky now swims."

"I knew about that," Grammy said. "I was there at the pool party that day." The three of them stood quietly for a minute. Off in the distance, an owl hooted.

"What am I going to do now?" Henry asked, collapsing to the ground in a heap. He buried his face in his hands. "I don't know what to do."

Grammy said, "This is hardly the end of it, Henry. It's more of a bump in the road." She reached down and patted his shoulder. "I have an idea, but I'll need some help."

CHAPTER TWENTY-NINE

$\mathcal{G}$rammy's plan wasn't the best one Paul had ever heard, but it was better than either one of them could come up with. Henry seemed relieved to let Grammy take charge, and Paul agreed to help.

Paul's part of the plan was simple: he went home and packed a small bag with some shorts and T-shirts and a pair of pajamas. He found an extra pair of shoes that he'd inherited from his cousin. They were still too big for him, but they would fit Henry, he thought. Paul filled a duffel bag with the clothes and threw in a spare toothbrush from the extras his mother kept in the medicine cabinet. His activity aroused Clem's curiosity. "Whatcha doing, Paul? Are you goin' somewhere?"

"It's not for me," Paul said. "Don't worry about it."

But Clem had already forgotten about it and was on to the next subject. "When I walk kinda fast my dog tags make a big noise, but when I go slow, not so much," Clem said and shook his head to illustrate.

"Okay," Paul said. Clem was getting on his nerves, but if he didn't answer, the dog just kept talking. Paul zipped the bag and left his room, walking quietly through the house so as not to attract attention. When he was sure no one was looking, he opened the back door and set the duffle bag on the porch.

He flicked the outside light on and off, a signal to Henry that he could now sneak up to the house to retrieve the bag. When Paul checked the porch fifteen minutes later, it was gone. Step one of Grammy's plan was complete.

When the phone rang an hour later, Paul's mother said, "I wonder who'd be calling us now?" It wasn't really that late, but it was unusual because they seldom got calls in the evening.

"Hello?" she said, getting up and walking out of the room so she wouldn't disturb Dad's television viewing. As she left the room Paul heard her say, "Mrs. Lovejoy, how nice to hear from you." Paul was tempted to follow her and listen in, but he didn't want to arouse any suspicion, so he stayed in the living room with his father.

A commercial came on, and Dad had just muted the TV when Mom returned to the room. "I just had the oddest call," she said. "Celia's grandmother asked for a favor, and of course I said yes, but I have to say that it took me by surprise."

"What is it?" Dad said.

"Apparently they have relatives visiting from out of town, and the relatives have a boy about Paul's age. They're a little short of space, so she wondered if the boy, his name is Henry, could stay here for a night or two. She said he'd bring over a sleeping bag and that he's a very nice boy. You don't mind, do you, Paul?"

"No," Paul said. "I don't mind."

Paul's father looked puzzled. "If he's going to be in a sleeping bag, why doesn't he just stay at their house? How much space does a sleeping bag require?"

"Ken, I don't know what to tell you," she said, sighing. "Mrs. Lovejoy said they were in a bind. She was so kind to me when I was a child, I could hardly say no."

"I'm not saying you made the wrong decision," Dad said. "It's a nice thing to do. I just wondered at the necessity of it all. Why don't they want him there? Maybe the kid starts fires or something."

"Oh, Ken, I'm sure that's not the case. He's probably a very nice boy. And he'll have more fun here than at the Lovejoys' house, I'm sure. He and Paul can go swimming and play in the woods."

"You've got a good heart, Leah," Dad said, reaching for the remote. "Between your sister Vicky showing up every day to go swimming and now this, I give you a lot of credit. You're practically a saint."

"It's really not that big of a deal," she said.

"A strange kid in the house would be a big deal for a lot of people. One more mouth to feed, another kid to keep track of."

"It's just one or two nights. We'll manage."

A half hour later there was a knock at the door. Paul eagerly answered and was stunned by Henry's transformation. Since he'd last seen them, Grammy had snuck Henry into the Lovejoy house and let him shower and change into Paul's clothes. Not only that, but she'd cut his hair short, shorter than Paul's even. Henry looked like a different person. Younger and unsure of himself. He stood on the welcome mat holding the duffle and a rolled-up sleeping bag, looking shy. Grammy kept a steadying hand on Henry's shoulder.

Paul stood speechless, until Grammy said, "May we come in, Paul?" Paul stepped aside and let them enter.

Paul's mother came up behind him. "Welcome, Henry," she said, almost a little too enthusiastically, Paul thought. "We're so happy to have you stay with us."

"Thank you, ma'am. I'm pleased to be invited."

"Such good manners!" Mom said. She turned to Grammy. "I think this is going to work out just fine, Mrs. Lovejoy."

"Leah, I can't tell you how happy I am that you agreed to have Henry here."

"Our pleasure." Mom gave Paul a nudge. "Why don't you boys run along? You can show Henry your room."

"Okay," Paul said, and they were off. As they went up the stairs, he heard Celia's grandmother explain that Henry was afraid of dogs. His mother said it was no problem; they'd keep Clem in the basement during his visit.

Up in Paul's room, Henry dropped the duffle and the sleeping bag on the floor. "Nice room," he said.

"Thanks," Paul said. "You can have the bed tonight, if you want."

"No thanks," Henry said. "I'm used to sleeping on the ground. The sleeping bag will be good. I don't mind."

"Well, if you don't mind," Paul said. "Anyway, by tomorrow you'll be on your way home and back to your own bed."

"I hope so."

Paul sat on the bed. "I was thinking," he said. "I'm wondering how it's going to work if you go back in time."

"What do you mean, how is it going to work?"

"I mean, then there will be two of you. And if you tell your younger self not to wish, there will still be two of you. How is that going to work? Won't your family be confused? And which one is the real you?"

Henry sat down next to him. "I don't even want to think about it. At least I won't be young forever, and I'll be back in my own world. I'll think of something when I get there." He didn't sound that confident, but Grammy's plan was all they had.

"I'm sure it will all be fine," Paul said. "I just wondered. Anyway, tomorrow everything will change for you, and that has to be a good thing no matter what."

CHAPTER THIRTY

*D*eep in the woods, Jasmine went in search of Mira. All day she'd kept up with things from a distance, listening in as Grammy met up with Paul and Henry in the woods, and waiting until Henry was safely inside the McClutchy house.

Finally, she decided to give Mira an update. Jasmine flew to the opening of the underground cave which was Mira's home. She made her way down a staircase made from slabs of stone. "Hello, Mira," she called out. "It's me, Jasmine."

Inside she heard voices and saw a glow of light. Oh good, she thought, Mira was here. Mira's voice wasn't happy, though, and whoever she was talking to was a mumbler.

As Jasmine entered the room, another fairy, Boyd, brushed past her as he headed out. "Hey, Boyd," she said, but he didn't look like he was in a good mood, and he didn't answer. "What's his problem?" Jasmine asked Mira, who sat at a table writing something in her book. The room was illuminated by the warm glow of a bowl of crystals in the center of the table.

Mira shrugged. "Just the usual Boyd stuff. He's got the easiest assignment in the neighborhood, and he still can't keep on top of things. I just don't know what to do with him anymore." She pointed. "Sit. I'm eager to hear how you've worked things out."

Jasmine pulled up a chair. "I think you'll be impressed by how I'm handling the whole ring situation."

"Hit me with it."

"It's a very simple plan, really, but brilliant."

"Hmmm," Mira said. "We'll just see about that. What have you got?"

Jasmine leaned forward, her wings fluttering in excitement. "Henry is staying in Paul's house as a guest, so he's now somewhere safe. Henry, Paul, and Grammy have this plan—"

"Grammy?" Mira interrupted. "Oh yes, the original Celia. I keep forgetting that she's old now. I knew her when she was just a girl, you know."

"I know," Jasmine said. "Anyway, they think they have a plan, but what they don't know is that their plan isn't really the right plan. I've got something better up my sleeve, and if everything goes the way I want, all of this will be fixed."

"This better be good," Mira said. "I can't even imagine what you've come up with."

"Oh it's good all right. This is how it will work." She leaned in and told Mira the entire scheme in hushed tones, ending with, "And that's what I came up with." She smiled in delight.

Mira sat back approvingly. "Pretty good, but of course, everything has to happen just perfectly or it won't work. I'll keep my wings crossed for you." The crystals in the bowl, feeding off Mira's good mood, glowed more brightly.

"Thanks, Mira." Jasmine smiled widely. "I'll let you know how it goes."

CHAPTER THIRTY-ONE

*E*arly the next morning, Paul's family was pulled out of their sleep by someone pounding on the front door. The whole family and Henry woke up with a start, jumped out of bed, and made their way to the front hall. Paul's dad opened the door to find Aunt Vicky dressed in her swimsuit, a towel and flotation noodle under her arm.

"Good morning," Aunt Vicky said brightly, peering through the screen. "I just came for a little morning swim. Don't worry about offering me anything to eat or drink. Just let me get to the pool. I'll be out of your way in a jiffy."

"Vicky," Paul's dad said, "do you have any idea what time it is? We were all sleeping."

"Ooops. Sorry about that." Aunt Vicky put a hand up to her mouth. "Tomorrow I'll just go around back and not bother you." She opened the screen door and let herself in. "Hi, Paul. Hi, Paul's friend." She extended her hand to Henry, who shook it.

"My name is Henry," he said.

"Nice to meet you, Henry. If you boys want to swim, I'd love some company." And then she walked through the house, her flip-flops flapping as she made her way to the back door. "Sorry about waking you up. Just go back to bed. Don't mind me at all."

"She's planning on coming back tomorrow?" Paul's dad hissed at his mother. "This is getting out of hand." His face turned the dark shade of red that always worried Paul because it meant his dad was getting angry.

"I know, Ken, I know, but what can I say? She paid for the pool."

"I don't care if she paid for the pool." His voice got louder with each word. "Having her come over every day is absolutely ridiculous."

"Shhhh." Paul's mother put a finger to her lips. "Not in front of our guest." She looked at Paul and Henry. "Why don't you two boys go back to sleep, or else get some breakfast? Your father and I need to talk."

Paul and Henry left the entryway, dressed, and got themselves breakfast. Through it all, Paul's parents squabbled. "Do they usually go on like this?" Henry asked, taking a bite of jelly toast. The couple had moved their argument to the living room, but their voices carried.

Paul shook his head. "They usually get along okay. And now that my mom doesn't get her headaches, she's been in a really good mood."

"It's the ring," Henry said glumly. "It makes everyone miserable."

"Not me and Clem," Paul said. "We're both pretty happy with what we can do." To illustrate he stood up and levitated a foot above the floor. "Flying is the coolest thing ever. Later today, after you leave, I'm going to go out flying all over the neighborhood. Maybe this time I'll try going higher."

"You're going to get yourself killed," Henry said. "Or shot down."

"Not likely," Paul said. "I'm careful."

"I thought I was careful too, and look what happened." He took a sip of orange juice. "This juice is so good. I haven't had any for at least five years."

The boys were scheduled to meet Celia and her grandmother in the woods at eleven o'clock sharp. They kept their eyes on the clock, Henry eager to go home, and Paul eager to have him gone. Not that he disliked him, just that he wanted to have his life back. And the thought of flying again made him itchy with excitement.

Right before eleven Paul went to his room to get the ring. On his way outside he interrupted his parents' heated conversation to let them know he was leaving. "Mom? Dad? Henry and I are going to play in the woods, okay?"

They barely noticed him. "Fine," his mother said, not even looking his way. She poked a finger at his father's chest. "What do you want me to do? Tell her she can't come over anymore?"

Paul slipped out of the room and ran outside to the backyard where Henry waited. "Let's go," he said. "It's almost time."

They passed the pool where Aunt Vicky waved and splashed in their direction. "Boys! The water feels wonderful. Why don't you join me?"

"We will later, Aunt Vicky," Paul said. "We have to meet some friends in the woods."

"I don't know why you'd want to do anything else but swim," she said. "The water is glorious."

"Later," Paul said, gesturing to the woods. "We have to get going now. Bye, Aunt Vicky."

"Good-bye, Paul. Good-bye, Henry." She took a deep breath, pinched her nose, and bobbed below the surface.

"That's a lady with one serious problem," Henry said as they made their way through the woods.

"What do you mean?"

"She's addicted to swimming."

Paul paused. "I don't think a person can be addicted to swimming."

"Well, she is, mark my words. This is a classic example of the ring taking a good thing and making it completely awful."

When they got to the agreed upon meeting place, the Triple Trees, Grammy and Celia were already waiting. Grammy smiled widely when she saw the boys arrive. "Right on the dot," she said. "Very good, boys."

"I would have come earlier," Henry said. "I could have done this yesterday."

"What's going on, Grammy?" Celia asked, looking up at her grandmother. "What are we doing here?"

"You didn't tell her?" Henry said. "Oh great."

"Shush, Henry," Celia's grandmother said. "I wanted her to meet you first, and then I thought I would explain."

Henry let out a breath in an impatient huff.

Grammy leaned over to get closer to her granddaughter. "Celia, this very charming young man is Henry. He has an enormous problem, and only you can help him. I'm going to ask you to do something for me, if you would."

"Sure, Grammy, anything."

"You have to trust me, and repeat the words exactly as I say them."

Celia nodded, her eyes solemn. "What's his problem?"

Paul said, "His problem is that he never gets any older. He's been our age for like forever."

"Really?" Celia looked from Paul to her grandmother, not sure what to believe.

Grammy nodded. "It's true. Henry and I were the same age until he made a wish to be young forever. Then I got older and he stayed the same."

"He wished on this ring." Paul pulled it from his pocket and handed it to Celia, who regarded it intently. "It gives you abilities, like superhuman abilities. You get your greatest desire." His eyes shone brightly. "I wished I could fly, and now I can, Celia. It's the most amazing feeling ever."

"You get your wish, all right," Henry said bitterly. "Except it backfires on you. If you wish for something for yourself, it all turns sour. Only selfless wishes work out."

"We don't need to get into all that," Grammy said. "The important thing is that Celia will make a wish that helps you out. Can you do that, honey?"

But Celia wasn't listening to her grandmother because she was stuck on what Paul had said. "You can fly, really?" She held up the ring. "You wished on this ring, and now you can fly?"

"Yes, I can." To prove it, he fluttered up in the air and floated in a circle around the group.

"Show-off," Henry said.

"Paul, that's enough for now," Grammy said impatiently. "We need to concentrate on Henry's problem."

"Wow, that's amazing," Celia said, clapping loudly.

"That's nothing," Paul said, landing next to her. "I flew all the way home from Alex's house the other day. I was up near the clouds, and I went over your house. I could have sat on the roof if I wanted. The whole world looks incredible from up there."

"Oh, you're so lucky," Celia said. And then she said to her grandmother, "Can you believe he can fly?"

"That's not all, Celia. Clem talks now," Paul said. "He only talks to me so far, but I bet he'd talk to you. He really likes you."

"No kidding? Clem can talk?" Celia's eyes widened in amazement.

"I'm dead serious. He doesn't talk about anything interesting, he just yammers on and on about his water dish and what things smell like, but he talks just as clear as anything. You can understand every word."

Celia grinned. "This is like a good dream. You were right, Grammy, I did have to see it to believe it." She slipped the ring on her finger. "And look, it fits me perfectly. And I know exactly what I'm going to wish for now that it's my turn."

"It's not your turn," Henry said. "You don't get a wish. Your wish is supposed to help me get back to my family."

Celia's face clouded. "But I thought I could get my greatest desire. That's what Paul said."

"No," said Henry, stamping his foot. "That's not what we're doing here." He turned to Grammy. "This is a terrible plan. You were supposed to prepare her for her role in this matter. I never should have trusted you."

Grammy held up a hand. "Everyone just calm down."

"Don't talk to my grandmother that way," Celia said and poked a finger into Henry's chest. Henry grabbed at Celia, who wriggled out of his grasp.

"Stop it, both of you," cried out Grammy, but no one was listening to her, and now Paul had joined the fray, trying to push Henry away from Celia. Paul was strong, but years of living on his own had made Henry stronger. He threw Paul aside, and Paul landed against the trunk of the tree with a thunk. Celia screamed as Henry lunged toward her. And then, in a split second, she was gone.

CHAPTER THIRTY-TWO

"Where did she go?" Henry said. Where Celia had been standing was now nothing but air. The clearing suddenly got quiet. Grammy stood in shock, and Paul looked around and rubbed his head. "Seriously, where did she go?" Henry asked again.

"I have a very bad feeling about this," Grammy said. She cupped her hands around her mouth. "Celia? Celia!"

"I'm right here, Grammy." They could hear her voice, just a few feet from where they stood, but they still couldn't see her. Celia giggled a little. It was a creepy sound, coming out of nothing.

"Celia, you're invisible," Paul said.

"I know," Celia said. "It's what I wished for. I've always wanted to have an invisibility cloak like in *Harry Potter*, but this is even better because I don't need the cloak." Looking in the direction of her voice, Paul was able to see the ring still on Celia's finger, floating in midair. It was the only thing about her that wasn't invisible.

"But Celia," her grandmother said, "you're invisible permanently. I don't know how we're going to change you back.

How are we going to explain this to your parents? How will you go to school?"

"Oh." Celia's voice got quiet. "I didn't think of that."

"Oh, isn't this just precious," Henry said bitterly. "The princess gets her wish, and I'm still stuck here."

"Quiet, Henry," Grammy said. "This isn't just about you anymore. I've got a more serious issue now. I can't have a granddaughter who's invisible. We have to think of a way out of this."

"She did it to herself," Henry said. "I say you let her live with it."

"Yes, she did it to herself. She made a bad wish. You did the same yourself, so try to be compassionate." Grammy rubbed her forehead and sighed. "Everyone think hard and try to come up with a solution."

"Maybe we could paint me all over?" Celia said. "Then people could see me."

Henry smirked. "Sure, that will work."

Grammy said, "No need for sarcasm, Henry. I'm open to any and all suggestions. Celia dear, I think painting you would be a good short-term solution, but we're looking for an actual fix."

A slight breeze brought the scent of pine and the sound of birds chattering. There were big problems in the clearing, but around them nature went on as usual.

After a few minutes, Paul said, "What if I go get my friend Alex and we ask him to make a wish to undo it?"

"Gee, that sounds familiar. Oh right, that was today's plan," Henry said, "and I don't see that it turned out so well."

Celia said, "Maybe the fairies could help, Grammy. Remember how Mira guided me before when we had the problem with the house?"

"Oh darling, I think we've been over this. Fairy magic guides people, it can't *make* things happen. Mira can't help us with this."

"But couldn't we ask?" Celia said, and then she started to cry, little sniffles at first and then sobs that came out in gulps. Her grandmother reached out, and Celia, still invisible, walked into her arms. Paul watched as Grammy stroked a head no one could see.

"There's no point in asking," Grammy said. "We need to figure this out on our own."

This was the second time Paul had heard them talk about fairies, and they still hadn't explained it to him. "How come I never heard about the fairies?" Paul asked, tilting his head to one side.

"It's a long story," Grammy said. "We'll tell you about it another time."

Celia sniffed, and her voice came through the air. "I'm sorry, Grammy. I'm so sorry."

"I know, honey," Grammy said. "It's all right. Everyone makes mistakes. It's my fault for not preparing you properly."

"This is a touching scene and all," Henry said, "but we're no closer to figuring out a solution."

"Maybe you could live with my family," Paul said to him. "We could tell my parents you're an orphan or something so they'd let you stay. I would share my room with you."

Henry sighed. "That's very nice of you, Paul, but eventually you'd get older and taller and I never would. Your mom and dad would certainly know something was up when that happened. I appreciate the thought, though."

"Maybe a doctor could you give you a growth hormone or something," invisible Celia said through her sobs.

"It's not really a medical issue," Henry said.

Grammy held Celia tightly then looked up at Paul and said, "Perhaps you should get your friend Alex. We'll do it differently this time. We won't let him hold the ring until he understands what he's supposed to do." She took the ring off Celia's finger and handed it to Paul, who put it in his pocket.

"Do you really think bringing another person into this mess is a good idea?" Henry asked.

"If you have a better idea, I'd like to hear it," she said.

CHAPTER THIRTY-THREE

No one had a better idea, least of all Henry, who'd had sixty-five years to think about it. Celia, Henry, and Grammy agreed to wait in the woods, while Paul went home to call Alex. "Come right back and tell us what he says," Grammy said.

"Grammy," Celia said, "couldn't we ask my mom and dad to unwish for me?"

"Oh honey, I hate to get them involved if we can avoid it. They'd never trust me again. Kids are better with wishes. They know the magic is out there. Adults are a little behind in that area."

Paul ran as fast as he could through the woods, and then, remembering he could fly, he lifted off and soared for the last stretch. When he got to the edge of the woods, he dropped down and walked the remaining way to his backyard. After being airborne, walking was excruciatingly slow, like being a baby again and having to crawl. He vowed to fly whenever he had the chance.

Aunt Vicky was still in the pool doing the back crawl, and she waved a hand as he went past. Or maybe it was just part of the backstroke, hard to tell. He waved back anyway, just in case. Inside, his parents were still talking in the living room. The worst of the argument was over with, but they still didn't sound happy.

"Paul? Is that you?" his mother asked from the next room.

"Yeah, Mom, I'm just calling Alex to see if he wants to come over," he said, which seemed to satisfy her.

"Okay. Would you let the dog out?" she said.

Paul opened the basement door, and Clem came lazily up the stairs to meet him. "Thanks, Paul. Bout time someone remembered," the dog said appreciatively. He ambled through the kitchen to the doggie door and headed outside.

The phone call went as well as could be expected. Alex answered on the second ring and, after checking with his mom, said sure, he'd come right over and would bring his swim trunks. "Come as soon as you can. It's really important," Paul said, wrapping up the conversation. Good old Alex. Paul knew he'd come through for him.

Heading out the back door, he felt euphoric. When Clem came trotting up to him, Paul even paused to pat his head.

Clem yawned and said, "Where ya goin', Paul? Can I come?"

"Sorry, pal. I've got a little magic ring problem to solve, and you'd just get in the way."

Clem cocked his head to one side. "What's wrong with the ring?"

"What do you care? You never listen anyway," Paul said.

"Oh, don't be that way. All I wanna know is what's wrong with the ring."

Paul walked quickly past the pool, and Clem scrambled to keep up. Paul knew if he didn't answer, Clem would keep following him. Better to get it over with. "There's nothing wrong with the ring," he said, "but the magic is messing up everything. It's all getting pretty intense. Celia is invisible, and Henry has been a kid for more than sixty years. And Aunt Vicky—"

"What about Aunt Vicky?"

The voice startled him. Paul turned to see his Aunt Vicky, a brightly striped towel draped over her arm. He stopped, stunned to see her out of the pool. "Hi, Aunt Vicky," he said, his voice suddenly squeaky. "I thought you were swimming."

"I saw you talking to the dog." She pulled off her swimming cap, revealing red ridges across her forehead. "It made me curious, so I got out of the pool to see what was going on."

"Sometimes I like to talk to Clem."

"And sometimes he talks back?" She looked from Paul to Clem and back again, but both were silent. "That's what I heard. Or is this some kind of ventriloquist trick?"

"It's a long story," Paul said weakly. "I have to get back to my friends. Can we talk about this later?"

"I think talking about it now would be better," she said firmly. "You were saying that Celia is invisible and Henry has been a kid for sixty years. What do you mean?"

"It's a game we're playing," Paul said. "Just a goofy game." He looked back at the woods, hoping for a little help. If only Henry or one of the others would call his name, he'd have an excuse to get going. "And dogs don't talk, you know that, Aunt Vicky. That would be silly." As if to agree, Clem shook his head and lay down on the grass next to Paul. "I don't want to be rude, Aunt Vicky, but I really have to get back to my friends. They're waiting." The words were no sooner out of his mouth when he felt himself lift off the ground and move toward the woods. He was flying, but it wasn't him doing it himself. Something else was making it happen.

"Paul, what's going on?" Aunt Vicky said, her voice getting louder. "Come back."

He twisted his head to yell back, "I can't come back. I'm not doing this. I have no control of the situation." He rose higher and higher and zipped around in dizzying circles. What was happening? This was not the fun kind of flying he'd experienced before. The movement made him feel nauseated, and he wondered how far vomit would spread if he threw up while spinning around.

"Paul, Paul!" Aunt Vicky's voice yelled frantically, and Clem joined her by yowling, "Paaaauuuulll," like he was howling at the moon.

"I'm sorry. I can't help it," he hollered. He found himself flying through the woods, not in a direct line, but circling around trees and zigzagging back and forth, as if the magic were angry and shaking him about. He suddenly knew what Henry meant when he said the magic eventually backfired for everyone.

CHAPTER THIRTY-FOUR

By the time Paul reached the others in the woods, he was dizzy from being whipped around. He landed by crashing at Henry's feet. Grammy and Celia exclaimed in concern, and even Henry said, "Paul, are you all right?"

Paul sat up slowly, rubbing his head and trying to get the spinning to stop. He closed his eyes for a moment, but that made it worse. "I think I'm okay," he said slowly.

Henry helped him up, and Grammy let go of Celia to check him over. "Nothing broken I hope," she said.

Paul brushed off his shorts. "Just a little banged up."

"You really shouldn't go so fast." Celia's voice came through the air. "That was crazy fast."

"I couldn't help it," Paul said. "I had no control of anything. I thought I was going to die."

"There are worse things than that," Henry said.

Paul pulled the ring out of his pocket, put it on his finger, and studied it intently. "This thing is wicked. I can see why someone buried it underground."

"A little while ago you thought it was the best thing since sliced bread," Henry said smugly.

"I changed my mind."

Off in the distance they heard the sound of people and a dog approaching. "Paul? Paul?" It was Paul's mother and Aunt Vicky, and they were accompanied by Clem, who took turns barking and howling, "Paaauuuullll," as if the name had multiple syllables.

"Now what?" Grammy said, sighing.

"Did you tell them?" Henry asked, grabbing Paul's arm because he was afraid of Clem.

"No, I swear I didn't say—" He wasn't able to finish because the two women charged into the clearing, their faces red and breathing hard.

"Oh," Paul's mother said. "Oh, thank goodness you're all right, Paul. Your aunt gave me the scare of my life." She gave him a hug, squishing him so tightly against her front that he had trouble breathing. "She said some strange force had dragged you off." And then, noticing Celia's grandmother, she said, "Hello, Mrs. Lovejoy."

Paul squirmed out of her grasp. "Let go, Mom. You're squeezing me too hard."

"He gets so embarrassed when I hug him in public," she said to the others. She reached over and ruffled his hair. "You know how boys are." She turned to his aunt. "Vicky, you gave me such a fright. I think you've been spending too much time in the pool. The chlorine is affecting your eyesight."

"It's not my eyesight," Vicky said, sputtering. "I saw him get pulled into the air by something, I don't know what. And didn't you hear the dog calling his name?" They all looked at

Clem, who sat down abruptly and took a sudden interest in his own butt. "The dog talks, I tell you," Vicky said. "I heard it with my own ears. I've figured this whole thing out. It's that ring you had before, the one you let me wear at the pool party. It's magic, and it's causing all kinds of problems."

"Oh Vicky, don't be silly," Mom said. "A magic ring? Do you realize how ridiculous that sounds? Besides, that ring is lost, thanks to you, I might add."

"It's not lost," Vicky said. "Paul has it on his finger right now."

Paul stuck his hand behind his back, but it was too late. His mother couldn't be fooled. "Paul," she said sternly, "do you have that ring?"

He hung his head but didn't say anything. Henry and Grammy held their breath.

"Paul," his mother said again, "hand it over." He slowly pulled it off his finger and set it in her outstretched hand. She put it on her finger. "I can't believe you had it and didn't tell me about it. I never thought my son would lie to me."

A wave of guilt washed over Paul. "I didn't lie to you, Mom. I just didn't tell you I found it again."

"Avoiding the truth is pretty much the same thing as lying," she said sadly. "I don't know if I can trust you ever again, Paul." She blinked back tears. This was so much worse than if she'd gotten mad. He could handle yelling and being grounded, but seeing his mother cry was unbearable.

"I'm sorry, Mom," Paul said, on the verge of crying himself. He was sorrier than he'd ever been in his life, not that being sorry helped.

"I was so excited when I found this ring," she said, "but now the sight of it makes me sick. I'm not going to be keeping it, I can tell you that much. And I'm not giving it to anyone I know," she said, turning to Aunt Vicky. "I want it gone."

The whole group was silent. Paul could hear Celia shuffling her feet anxiously, but luckily she didn't say a word. What would happen to all of them if his mother sold the ring? If only there was a way to undo the whole thing. If only. Paul squinted and thought hard. And then an idea struck him. But he had to act quickly.

"Mom," he said, "if you could have any wish, any wish in the world, would you wish this ring never existed and that everything was back to the way it was originally?"

"That's exactly what I'd wish," she said, taking a tissue offered by Celia's grandmother and dabbing her eyes. "Darn ring. Nothing but trouble."

"Could you say it?" Paul said.

"Say what?" She blew her nose.

"What I just said. Could you say it yourself?"

"What a good idea to wish the ring never existed," Grammy said, and Henry nodded, his eyes bright. "I wish I'd thought of that."

"I don't know what difference it would make," Mom said. "What's done is done."

"Words have power," Grammy said, "even when you don't think they do. It would probably make us all feel better if you'd just repeat what he said."

"Please, Mom, would you?" Paul said. "Say: I wish this ring never existed and that everything was back to normal, the way it's supposed to be."

His mother looked around at the group, shrugged, and then gave in. "Okay, if it will make you happy. I wish this ring never existed and that everything was back to normal, the way it's supposed to be."

CHAPTER THIRTY-FIVE

Nothing rumbled or roared. There was no whoosh or sparkles flying through the air. Paul felt exactly the same, but in the space of time it took to wink, Celia appeared next to her grandmother and Henry disappeared. Aunt Vicky was gone too, leaving Celia, her grandmother, Paul, and his mother standing under the shade of the Triple Trees. Celia looked down at her feet and happily examined her hands. She gave Paul a wide smile. It worked!

Paul's mother was confused. "What was I just saying?" she asked, looking to Grammy for help.

"Celia and I were just heading back to our house," Grammy said, "and you were asking Paul to come home because his friend Alex will be arriving soon."

"Oh yes," Mom said, smiling. "That's exactly it. I'm so forgetful lately. I think I'd lose my head if it weren't attached."

"We all go through that," Grammy said. "Don't worry about it." She put her arm around Celia's shoulders. "Time to go. Your mother will be looking for us."

After they'd left, Paul asked, "Where's Aunt Vicky?"

"At home, I would assume," Mom replied. "Why do you ask?"

"I thought she was here." His forehead scrunched in confusion.

"Here? Why would she be here?"

"Because she came to swim this morning," Paul said.

"Vicky? Oh, don't be silly. You know she doesn't swim." She reached over and ruffled his hair. "Why would you say such a thing?"

"I don't know," Paul said. "I just thought she might have changed her mind."

"That's never going to happen, believe me. No, you boys will have the pool to yourselves today."

* * *

Henry found himself standing in front of his house dressed exactly as he was the day he made the wish. But of course, there was no wish, because the ring had never existed. He stood with the nagging feeling *something* had happened, but he couldn't quite remember what it was. Funny, it seemed significant, but no matter how hard he tried, nothing came to mind. It was like the wisp of a dream that faded within moments of awakening.

Huh.

His mother came out of the house, a broom in hand. "Henry? Why are you standing there, boy? Are you already done with your chores?"

Ah yes, his chores. He still had to do them. "No, Ma, I haven't even started them yet."

She frowned. "Get a move on then. The eggs aren't magically going to collect themselves, you know. You have to do the work."

"I know, I know."

His mother began sweeping the porch. Determination lit her face as she concentrated on her task. Henry felt a surge of affection. She worked so hard, but never complained. "Ma?" he said.

She paused. "Yes?"

"I love you."

His mother smiled broadly. "I love you too, my son." She waved the broom in his direction. "But you still have to do your chores."

"I know. I just wanted to tell you."

CHAPTER THIRTY-SIX

*J*asmine and Boyd watched the scene from the tops of the Triple Trees. Mira had ordered Boyd to accompany Jasmine on this mission. "Let him see how a good fairy does the job," she'd said. Boyd had grumbled at having to go on this field trip, but his interest perked up when Celia became invisible, and he held his breath when Paul's mother repeated the words that fixed everything. When all four of the humans had left, he'd high-fived Jasmine and clapped enthusiastically.

"What a surprise. There's no way you could have seen that coming," Boyd said.

Jasmine sat down on the branch and leaned against the tree trunk. "What do you mean?"

"I mean, it was nice the way the human boy, Paul, figured out a solution on his own."

Jasmine tucked her hair behind her ear. "I'd hardly say he figured it out on his own." She raised one eyebrow. "He had some help."

"You mean this was all your idea?" Boyd couldn't hide his look of astonishment. "You thought of this? Absolutely brilliant."

"It was nothing," Jasmine said with a wave of her hand. "Any fairy could have thought of it." Secretly, though, she knew she'd done something exceptional. She simply didn't want to make a big deal of it. It was just her job. Human beings could hardly function on their own. Without fairy guidance, who knew what might happen?

"Well played, Miss J.," Boyd said, nodding approvingly. "I'm proud to know you."

Jasmine beamed. She didn't know this yet, but Boyd was a blabbermouth, and her victory today would be the talk of the Watchful Woods fairies for years to come. The fledglings would seek out her advice when they were in a tough spot, and she would be lauded for her good counsel. For today, though, all she had was the satisfaction of a job well done.

And that was plenty.

CHAPTER THIRTY-SEVEN

One sunny afternoon, Celia and Paul sat in the shade of the Triple Trees eating a picnic lunch. Paul's mother had put together a feast of sandwiches, grapes, and cookies, along with a thermos of lemonade. "Did you ever notice that food always tastes better when you eat it outside?" Celia asked.

Paul said, "It tastes the same to me." He looked around. "Hey, Celia, remember the other day when we were here with my mom and your Grammy?" She nodded. "Do you remember how we got here in the first place?"

Celia took a sip from her cup. "We walked, I guess."

"I know we walked, but I don't remember what happened before that."

"Nothing happened before that."

"Are you sure?" Paul scratched his head. "It seems like there was something. I just can't remember what it was."

"You invited Alex over to swim, remember?"

"Oh yeah. That must be it." They sat in silence, eating their peanut butter and jelly sandwiches. Grape jelly, just the way Paul liked. His mother had a knack for remembering

his favorites. When they were done eating, they cleaned up, putting everything in a bag she'd sent for that purpose. Leave a place as clean as you found it was his mother's motto.

Paul stood up and looked around the trees. "Celia, you know what would be cool? If we built a tree house around here. It could be our fort."

Celia brightened. "I bet my dad would help us build it."

"We could make a ladder to get up, and we could hang a rope off one of the branches and swing really high. Like flying." Paul waved his arms excitedly.

"If we were up in the tree house and no one knew we were up there, we could spy on anyone who came by. It would be like we were invisible," Celia said.

"It would be so cool," Paul said. "I don't know why we didn't think of this before." He loved this place, with the trees standing guard around them. He used to think living in his friend Alex's neighborhood would be better, but he'd changed his mind. When you lived in a house near the woods, there was no end to the possibilities.

THE END

ABOUT THE AUTHOR

Karen McQuestion grew up in Milwaukee, Wisconsin, the second of four girls. As the daughter of two schoolteachers, she was required to get good grades and stay out of trouble, which she did—for the most part. Later she got a really cool last name when she married Greg McQuestion. When they first met, she was intrigued by the fact that he danced like Steve Martin and looked like Harrison Ford in the Indiana Jones movies. Today he looks less like Harrison Ford except for his smile—a mysterious smirk. The dancing is the same. Now she writes books for both adults and kids, and is a bestselling author in Kindle. Two of her novels placed in the top 100 Customer Kindle books for 2010, based on sales and reader reviews. McQuestion lives in Hartland, Wisconsin, with her husband and three kids.

When ten-year-old Celia learns that her grandmother's entertaining tales of fairies are actually true, she finds herself drawn into their world. Chosen by a fairy named Mira, she must embark on a dangerous quest to save the fairies' home-and her own-from complete destruction. This magical story combines heart-pounding adventure with an underlying message about the power of ordinary kindness.